Among the great imaginative artists of the nineteenth century, MacDonald's unusual talents were recognized even in his own lifetime. And in fact, although he died nearly seventy years ago, his reputation has retained all its luster and shows no signs of dimming.

EVENOR represents the last of the Adult Fantasy he wrote—three shimmering tales, brought together here for the first time.

> "George MacDonald was a Scot of genius as genuine as Carlyle's; he could write fantasy that made all experience a fairy-tale. He could give the real sense that everyone had the end of an elfin thread that must at last lead them into Paradise."
>
> G. K. Chesterton

Other Adult Fantasy by
George MacDonald

PHANTASTES

LILITH

**Adult
Fantasy**

Available in Ballantine Book Editions

EVENOR

George MacDonald

With Introduction and Notes by
Lin Carter

BALLANTINE BOOKS
An Intext Publisher
NEW YORK • LONDON

BALLANTINE BOOKS, INC.
101 Fifth Avenue, New York, N.Y. 10003

This book is dedicated to the late C. S. Lewis, of Perelandra and of Narnia as much as of Oxford, who loved these tales so much that they left their mark on his mind, his life, and his writing, to the joy and enrichment of his own readers.

Contents

. . . Behind those world-enclosing hills
There sat a mighty woman, with a face
As calm as life, when its intensity
Pushes it nigh to death, waiting for him
To make him grand forever with a kiss
And send him silent through the toning worlds.

—George MacDonald: *A Hidden Life* (1857)

About EVENOR *and*
George MacDonald:

The Dubious Land

The major fantasies of George MacDonald occupy a dim mid-region between the kind of novel that, however fantastic and improbable it may be, is supposed to be taken seriously as a sequence of events which "really" happened, and the novel whose settings or characters or actions are meant to be read as symbols. In this mid-region, which I like to think of as "the dubious land," the fiction of George MacDonald reigns supreme.

In 1969, the year in which we launched our Adult Fantasy Series, we published MacDonald's masterpiece, *Lilith*.

In 1970 we brought into print again his second great fantasy novel, *Phantastes*.

It is largely upon these two famous "dream romances" that George MacDonald's reputation as a great mythopoeic artist must rest. He wrote no other full-length fantasy novels for adults.

But he did write a number of short prose narratives in much the same mood and style as his haunting dream romances. Some of these are fairy-stories obviously intended for children—"The Light Princess," "The Giant's Heart," and so on. But at least three of these shorter prose narratives are too serious, too meaningful, too beautifully told, to be ranked with his ventures into the invented fairy-tale.

These three works comprise this book. The major story, and also the longest, is "The Wise Woman." I was not aware of the existence of this tale until it was brought to my attention by one of my readers in Boston, who not only suggested it might be worthy of being included in the Series but was generous enough to lend me his copy so that I might read it for myself. I read it, liked it, and was delighted to see how well it would go together in a single book with the other two prose narratives MacDonald obviously intended for his grownup readers, "The Carasoyn" and "The Golden Key."

With the publication of this book we have exhausted the adult fantasy of George MacDonald. But those of you who find pleasure and excitement in his work need not despair. For we are launching a companion series to our Adult Fantasy editions, a series of classic fantasy novels for children which we have named "'Magic Kingdoms." Among the first of our Magic Kingdom books you will find George MacDonald's most famous children's fantasy novel, *The Princess and the Goblin*.

Each year, among our annual Magic Kingdom releases, we hope to include a George MacDonald fantasy, so that eventually we will have *all* of his fantasy, both adult and juvenile, in print at the same time.

MacDonald was an extraordinary writer whose unusual talents were recognized in his own lifetime, and although he died sixty-six years ago, his reputation has retained its luster all that time and shows no sign of dimming in the years ahead.

At the height of his career, say around 1865, MacDonald was one of the most celebrated writers of his age, and he knew everyone in the literary world. There exists a perfectly fascinating photograph (undated, but taken sometime before 1859) which shows a roomful of bearded gentlemen. Their names are rather famous—Dickens, Thackeray, Trollope, Wilkie Collins, Carlyle, Macaulay, Bulwer-Lytton, and George MacDonald. Had some anarchist planted a bomb in that room, timed to explode when the photograph was taken, the Victorian Age would thereafter have been a blank spot in the history of English literature.

MacDonald was on friendly terms with nearly every famous writer of his day. Lewis Carroll lent him the original unpublished manuscript of *Alice* and asked his opinion; John Ruskin made MacDonald his intimate confidant during an anguished courtship; Charles Kingsley suggested MacDonald for the chair of Rhetoric and Belles Lettres at Edinburgh; Tennyson dropped in on the MacDonalds to borrow books; Matthew Arnold and Leigh Hunt were friends of his. And when he came to America in 1872, the greatest living writers in the United States—Emerson, Longfellow and Whittier among them—gave him the warmest of welcomes.

Indeed, America took George MacDonald to its heart. A delegation of deacons from one of the big rich Fifth Avenue churches in New York called on him and begged him to accept the pastorate of their church for a perfectly astonishing annual salary—$20,000! It is fascinating to conjecture what MacDonald's life might have been had he accepted that princely paycheck and become a New Yorker.

Even after MacDonald returned to England he retained a very special place in the affections of his American friends. When Mark Twain visited England some years later, he came to call on the MacDonalds, stayed for a visit with them, and ever after remained a friend and admirer.

As he grew older, however, MacDonald's powers

declined, and prior to his death in 1905 at the age
of eighty-one he published nothing new for seven or
eight years. Enthusiastic admirers continued to
champion his cause and would not permit a fickle
public to forget him. The judgment of posterity has
placed him very high among the great English
writers of his time, and the writers who have come
after him have spoken out, decade after decade, in
praise of George MacDonald.

His greatest books, *Lilith* and *Phantastes,* have
never lacked admirers. Dickens, who rarely had a
good word for a competitor, praised *Phantastes*
highly, and H. G. Wells spoke in admiration of the
artistry and imagination of *Lilith*. When MacDonald
died, G. K. Chesterton composed his obituary, de-
claring, "If we test the matter by originality of atti-
tude, George MacDonald was one of the three or
four greatest men of the nineteenth century."

Throughout the more than half a century since
his death, the fantasies of George MacDonald have
continued to excite the intense adulation of other
fantasy writers. Chesterton, for example, was not
content with a mere word or two of praise in an
obituary but continued to speak and write on Mac-
Donald for years. Twenty years after he wrote that
obituary, Chesterton was still hailing MacDonald's
genius, calling him "St. Francis of Aberdeen," celebrating his best work as a "miracle of imagination,"
and devoting pages of praise on him in a study of
the authors of his day called *The Victorian Age in
Literature*. In our own day, C. S. Lewis and Roger
Lancelyn Green have labored with affection and
great dedication to keep the name of George Mac-
Donald alive. Indeed, Lewis edited a two-volume
anthology of selections from MacDonald's sermons.
And other modern writers, such as the poet W. H.
Auden, and fantasy novelists like Charles Williams
and J. R. R. Tolkien have, in the words of Robert

Lee Wolff, "paid MacDonald the even greater compliment of presenting his ideas in twentieth-century fantasies—often influenced by his creations—without explicit acknowledgement."

But among them all, C. S. Lewis stands out as MacDonald's greatest disciple in our own day. Indeed, Lewis wrote of his own personal debt to MacDonald:

> "I have never concealed the fact that I regarded him as my master; indeed I fancy I have never written a book in which I did not quote from him. But it has not seemed to me that those who have received my books kindly take even now sufficient notice of the affiliation. Honesty drives me to emphasize it."

Because of his love for MacDonald, I have taken the liberty of dedicating my edition of MacDonald's shorter adult prose fantasies—to which I have given the title *Evenor*—to C. S. Lewis.

This title deserves a word of explanation itself.

The Athenian philosopher, Plato, in one of his more celebrated dialogues, recorded or perhaps invented the myth of Evenor. In Plato, he is the first man, the Adam of the philosophers, sprung from the earth itself at the beginning of all things. "Evenor the Earth-born," Plato calls him.

This symbol of the earth as parent and progenitor of mankind, from which we mortals all descend, seems to me an admirable notion and one that would have pleased George MacDonald, for his own fiction —filled as it is with metaphor and mysticism and symbols of a comparable nature—frequently employs similar ideas. Indeed, MacDonald sees terrestrial nature as a maternal or paternal figure, and his stories, which contain numerous enigmatic and mysterious figures of divine authority, almost seem to share this element of Platonic mysticism.

In 1924, celebrating the centennial of George MacDonald's birth, a leading article in the *Times Literary Supplement* had this to say of George Mac-Donald:

> "The author of *David Elginbrod* and *Robert Falconer* and *Alec Forbes* was a good novelist. The poet of the *Poems* and *The Diary of an Old Soul* was a true poet . . . [But] the author of *The Golden Key* and of *Lilith* had a touch of genius. Not yet has he been recognized as the man who did one sort of work better than anyone else has ever done it . . . the writing of what are commonly called fairy-stories."

Since those words were written, MacDonald has been given his true place among the great imaginative artists who laid the foundations for the modern world of fantasy literature. Today he is recognized as a forerunner among those authors who have created the imaginary-world fantasy, and as one of the greatest.

In that dim country I call the dubious land, that lies between the "waking world" of realistic writing and the shadowy region of pure allegory, George MacDonald was the first pioneer. There in the dubious land he found his heart's home. And he made of the dubious land his own private kingdom.

May it be a long, long time before he is dethroned.

—LIN CARTER
Editorial Consultant
The Ballantine Adult Fantasy Series

Hollis, Long Island, New York

The first of our three tales by George MacDonald is almost long enough to be considered a novel in its own right, 35,800 words in length. Indeed, unlike the two tales that follow it, *The Wise Woman* was first published as a single book (in London by the firm of Strahan). It appeared on the bookstalls of London in 1875, three years after the publication of *The Princess and the Goblin* and seven years before that book's sequel, *The Princess and Curdie,* would appear.

I wonder what its first readers made of it. No doubt they bought it thinking it would have the same magic and wonder they had found in the first Curdie book. Yet, although it bears the traditional form of the fairy-tale, it was obviously not meant for children, for the undercurrents of *The Wise Woman* are too deep and powerful for the young. It remains a strange and baffling book, filled with black shadows and glimmering shapes.

The Wise Woman was published in the United States by Dodd & Mead, as the firm was then known, and under a different title: *A Double Story*. A reader in Boston named Steve Bradley not only called this story to my attention, but also very generously lent me his own copy to read, for which I am very grateful.

The Wise Woman

I

There was a certain country where things used to go rather oddly. For instance, you could never tell whether it was going to rain or hail, or whether or not the milk was going to turn sour. It was impossible to say whether the next baby would be a boy, or a girl, or even, after he was a week old, whether he would wake sweet-tempered or cross.

In strict accordance with the peculiar nature of this country of uncertainties, it came to pass one day, that in the midst of a shower of rain that might well be called golden, seeing the sun, shining as it fell, turned all its drops into molten topazes, and every drop was good for a grain of golden corn, or a yellow cowslip, or a buttercup, or a dandelion at least;—while this splendid rain was falling, I say, with a musical patter upon the great leaves of the horse-chestnuts, which hung like Vandyke collars about the necks of the creamy, red-spotted blossoms, and on the leaves of the sycamores, looking as if they had blood in their veins, and on a multitude of flowers, of which some stood up and boldly held out their cups to catch their share, while others cowered down, laughing, under the soft patting blows of the heavy warm drops;—while this lovely rain was washing all the air clean from the motes, and the bad odors, and the poison-seeds that had escaped from their prisons during the long drought; —while it fell, splashing and sparkling, with a hum,

and a rush, and a soft clashing—but stop! I am
stealing, I find, and not that only, but with clumsy
hands spoiling what I steal:—

O Rain! with your dull twofold sound,
The clash hard by, and the murmur all round:

—there! take it, Mr. Coleridge;—while, as I was
saying, the lovely little rivers whose fountains are the
clouds, and which cut their own channels through
the air, and make sweet noises rubbing against their
banks as they hurry down and down, until at length
they are pulled up on a sudden, with a musical
plash, in the very heart of an odorous flower, that
first gasps and then sighs up a blissful scent, or on
the bald head of a stone that never says, Thank
you;—while the very sheep felt it blessing them,
though it could never reach their skins through the
depth of their long wool, and the veriest hedgehog—
I mean the one with the longest spikes—came and
spiked himself out to impale as many of the drops as
he could;—while the rain was thus falling, and the
leaves, and the flowers, and the sheep, and the
cattle, and the hedgehog, were all busily receiving
the golden rain, something happened. It was not a
great battle, nor an earthquake, nor a coronation,
but something more important than all those put
together. *A baby-girl was born;* and her father was a
king; and her mother was a queen; and her uncles
and aunts were princes and princesses; and her first-
cousins were dukes and duchesses; and not one of
her second-cousins was less than a marquis or mar-
chioness, or of their third-cousins less than an earl or
countess: and below a countess they did not care to
count. So the little girl was Somebody; and yet for
all that, strange to say, the first thing she did was to
cry. I told you it was a strange country.

As she grew up, everybody about her did his best

to convince her that she was Somebody; and the girl herself was so easily persuaded of it that she quite forgot that anybody had ever told her so, and took it for a fundamental, innate, primary, first-born, self-evident, necessary, and incontrovertible idea and principle that *she was Somebody*. And far be it from me to deny it. I will even go so far as to assert that in this odd country there was a huge number of Somebodies. Indeed, it was one of its oddities that every boy and girl in it was rather too ready to think he or she was Somebody; and the worst of it was that the princess never thought of there being more than one Somebody—and that was herself.

Far away to the north in the same country, on the side of a bleak hill, where a horse-chestnut or a sycamore was never seen, where were no meadows rich with buttercups, only steep, rough, breezy slopes, covered with dry prickly furze and its flowers of red gold, or moister, softer broom with its flowers of yellow gold, and great sweeps of purple heather, mixed with bilberries, and crowberries, and cranberries—no, I am all wrong: there was nothing out yet but a few furze-blossoms; the rest were all waiting behind their doors till they were called; and no full, slow-gliding river with meadow-sweet along its oozy banks, only a little brook here and there, that dashed past without a moment to say, "How do you do?"—there (would you believe it?) while the same cloud that was dropping down golden rain all about the queen's new baby was dashing huge fierce handfuls of hail upon the hills, with such force that they flew spinning off the rocks and stones, went burrowing in the sheep's wool, stung the cheeks and chin of the shepherd with their sharp spiteful little blows, and made his dog wink and whine as they bounded off his hard wise head, and long sagacious nose; only, when they dropped plump down the chimney, and fell hissing in the little fire, they caught it then, for the clever little fire soon sent them up the chimney again, a good deal swollen, and harmless enough for a while, there (what do you think?) among the hailstones, and the heather, and the cold mountain air, another little girl was born, whom the shepherd her father, and the shepherdess her mother, and a good many of her kindred too, thought Somebody. She had not an uncle or an aunt that was less than a shepherd or dairymaid, not a cousin that was less than a farm-laborer, not a second-cousin that was less than a grocer, and they did not count farther. And yet (would you believe it?) she too cried the very first thing. It *was* an odd country! And, what is still more surprising, the shepherd and shepherdess and the dairymaids and the laborers were not a bit wiser than the king and the queen and the dukes and the marquises and the earls; for they too, one and all, so constantly taught the little woman that she was Somebody, that she also forgot that there were a great many more Somebodies besides herself in the world.

It was, indeed, a peculiar country, very different from ours—so different, that my reader must not be too much surprised when I add the amazing fact, that most of its inhabitants, instead of enjoying the things they had, were always wanting the things they had not, often even the things it was least likely they ever could have. The grown men and women being like this, there is no reason to be further astonished that the Princess Rosamond—the name her parents gave her because it means *Rose of the World*—should grow up like them, wanting every thing she could and every thing she couldn't have. The things she could have were a great many too many, for her foolish parents always gave her what they could; but still there remained a few things they couldn't give her, for they were only a common king and queen. They could and did give her a lighted candle when she cried for it, and managed by much care that she should not burn her fingers or set her frock on fire; but when she cried for the moon, that they could not give her. They did the worst thing possible, instead, however; for they pretended to do what they could not. They got her a thin disc of brilliantly polished silver, as near the size of the moon as they could agree upon; and, for a time she was delighted.

But, unfortunately, one evening she made the discovery that her moon was a little peculiar, inasmuch as she could not shine in the dark. Her nurse happened to snuff out the candles as she was playing with it; and instantly came a shriek of rage, for her moon had vanished. Presently, through the opening of the curtains, she caught sight of the real moon, far away in the sky, and shining quite calmly, as if she had been there all the time; and her rage increased to such a degree that if it had not passed off in a fit, I do not know what might have come of it.

As she grew up it was still the same, with this difference, that not only must she have every thing, but she got tired of every thing almost as soon as she had it. There was an accumulation of things in her nursery and schoolroom and bedroom that was perfectly appalling. Her mother's wardrobes were almost useless to her, so packed were they with things of which she never took any notice. When she was five years old, they gave her a splendid gold repeater, so close set with diamonds and rubies, that the back was just one crust of gems. In one of her little tempers, as they called her hideously ugly rages, she dashed it against the back of the chimney, after which it never gave a single tick; and some of the diamonds went to the ash-pit. As she grew older still, she became fond of animals, not in a way that brought them much pleasure, or herself much satisfaction. When angry, she would beat them, and try to pull them to pieces, and as soon as she became a little used to them, would neglect them altogether. Then, if they could, they would run away, and she was furious. Some white mice, which she had ceased feeding altogether, did so; and soon the palace was swarming with white mice. Their red eyes might be seen glowing, and their white skins gleaming, in every dark corner; but when it came to the king's finding a nest of them in his second-best crown, he was angry and ordered them to be drowned. The princess heard of it, however, and raised such a clamor, that there they were left until they should run away of themselves; and the poor king had to wear his best crown every day till then. Nothing that was the princess's property, whether she cared for it or not, was to be meddled with.

Of course, as she grew, she grew worse; for she never tried to grow better. She became more and more peevish and fretful very day—dissatisfied not only with what she had, but with all that was around her, and constantly wishing things in general to be different. She found fault with every thing and everybody, and all that happened, and grew more and more disagreeable to every one who had to do with her. At last, when she had nearly killed her nurse, and had all but succeeded in hanging herself, and was miserable from morning to night, her parents thought it time to do something.

A long way from the palace, in the heart of a deep wood of pine-trees, lived a wise woman. In some countries she would have been called a witch; but that would have been a mistake, for she never did any thing wicked, and had more power than any witch could have. As her fame was spread through all the country, the king heard of her; and, thinking she might perhaps be able to suggest something, sent for her. In the dead of the night, lest the princess should know it, the king's messenger brought into the palace a tall woman, muffled from head to foot

in a cloak of black cloth. In the presence of both
their Majesties, the king, to do her honor, requested
her to sit; but she declined, and stood waiting to
hear what they had to say. Nor had she to wait
long, for almost instantly they began to tell her the
dreadful trouble they were in with their only child;
first the king talking, then the queen interposing with
some yet more dreadful fact, and at times both letting out a torrent of words together, so anxious were
they to show the wise woman that their perplexity
was real, and their daughter a very terrible one. For
a long while there appeared no sign of approaching
pause. But the wise woman stood patiently folded in
her black cloak, and listened without word or motion. At length silence fell; for they had talked themselves tired, and could not think of any thing more
to add to the list of their child's enormities.

After a minute, the wise woman unfolded her
arms; and her cloak dropping open in front,
disclosed a garment made of a strange stuff, which
an old poet who knew her well has thus described:—

> All lilly white, withoutten spot or pride,
> That seemd like silke and silver woven neare;
> But neither silke nor silver therein did appeare.

"How very badly you have treated her!" said the
wise woman. "Poor child!"

"Treated her badly?" gasped the king.

"She is a very wicked child," said the queen; and
both glared with indignation.

"Yes, indeed!" returned the wise woman. "She is
very naughty indeed, and that she must be made to
feel; but it is half your fault too."

"What!" stammered the king. "Haven't we given
her every mortal thing she wanted?"

"Surely," said the wise woman: "what else could

have all but killed her? You should have given her a few things of the other sort. But you are far too dull to understand me."

"You are very polite," remarked the king, with royal sarcasm on his thin, straight lips.

The wise woman made no answer beyond a deep sigh; and the king and queen sat silent also in their anger, glaring at the wise woman. The silence lasted again for a minute, and then the wise woman folded her cloak around her, and her shining garment vanished like the moon when a great cloud comes over her. Yet another minute passed and the silence endured, for the smouldering wrath of the king and queen choked the channels of their speech. Then the wise woman turned her back on them, and so stood. At this, the rage of the king broke forth; and he cried to the queen, stammering in his fierceness,—

"How should such an old hag as that teach Rosamond good manners? She knows nothing of them herself! Look how she stands!—actually with her back to us."

At the word the wise woman walked from the room. The great folding doors fell to behind her; and the same moment the king and queen were quarrelling like apes as to which of them was to blame for her departure. Before their altercation was over, for it lasted till the early morning, in rushed Rosamond, clutching in her a hand a poor little white rabbit, of which she was very fond, and from which, only because it would not come to her when she called it, she was pulling handfuls of fur in the attempt to tear the squealing, pink-eared, red-eyed thing to pieces.

"Rosa, Rosa*mond!*" cried the queen; whereupon Rosamond threw the rabbit in her mother's face. The king started up in a fury, and ran to seize her. She darted shrieking from the room. The king rushed after her; but, to his amazement, she was nowhere to be seen: the huge hall was empty.—No: just outside the door, close to the threshold, with her back to it, sat the figure of the wise woman, muffled in her dark cloak, with her head bowed over her knees. As the king stood looking at her, she rose slowly, crossed the hall, and walked away down the marble staircase. The king called to her; but she never turned her head, or gave the least sign that she heard him. So quietly did she pass down the wide marble stair, that the king was all but persuaded he had seen only a shadow gliding across the white steps.

For the princess, she was nowhere to be found. The queen went into hysterics; and the rabbit ran away. The king sent out messengers in every direction, but in vain.

In a short time the palace was quiet—as quiet as it used to be before the princess was born. The king and queen cried a little now and then, for the hearts of parents were in that country strangely fashioned; and yet I am afraid the first movement of those very hearts would have been a jump of terror if the ears above them had heard the voice of Rosamond in one of the corridors. As for the rest of the household, they could not have made up a single tear amongst them. They thought, whatever it might be for the princess, it was, for every one else, the best thing that could have happened; and as to what had become of her, if their heads were puzzled, their hearts took no interest in the question. The lord-chancellor alone had an idea about it, but he was far too wise to utter it.

II

The fact, as is plain, was, that the princess had disappeared in the folds of the wise woman's cloak. When she rushed from the room, the wise woman caught her to her bosom and flung the black garment around her. The princess struggled wildly, for she was in fierce terror, and screamed as loud as choking fright would permit her; but her father, standing in the door, and looking down upon the wise woman, saw never a movement of the cloak, so tight was she held by her captor. He was indeed aware of a most angry crying, which reminded him of his daughter; but it sounded to him so far away, that he took it for the passion of some child in the street, outside the palace-gates. Hence, unchallenged, the wise woman carried the princess down the marble stairs, out at the palace-door, down a great flight of steps outside, across a paved court, through the brazen gates, along half-roused streets where people were opening their shops, through the huge gates of the city, and out into the wide road, vanishing northwards; the princess struggling and screaming all the time, and the wise woman holding her tight. When at length she was too tired to struggle or scream any more, the wise woman unfolded her cloak, and set her down; and the princess saw the light and opened her swollen eyelids. There was nothing in sight that she had ever seen before. City and palace had disappeared. They were upon a wide road going straight on, with a ditch on each side of it, that behind them widened into the great moat surrounding the city.

She cast up a terrified look into the wise woman's face, that gazed down upon her gravely and kindly. Now the princess did not in the least understand kindness. She always took it for a sign either of partiality or fear. So when the wise woman looked kindly upon her, she rushed at her, butting with her head like a ram; but the folds of the cloak had closed around the wise woman; and, when the princess ran against it, she found it hard as the cloak of a bronze statue, and fell back upon the road with a great bruise on her head. The wise woman lifted her again, and put her once more under the cloak, where she fell asleep, and where she awoke again only to find that she was still being carried on and on.

When at length the wise woman again stopped and set her down, she saw around her a bright moonlit night, on a wide heath, solitary and houseless. Here she felt more frightened than before; nor was her terror assuaged when, looking up, she saw a stern, immovable countenance, with cold eyes fixedly regarding her. All she knew of the world being derived from nursery-tales, she concluded that the wise woman was an ogress, carrying her home to eat her.

I have already said that the princess was, at this time of her life, such a low-minded creature, that severity had greater influence over her than kindness. She understood terror better far than tenderness. When the wise woman looked at her thus, she fell on her knees, and held up her hands to her, crying,—

"Oh, don't eat me! don't eat me!"

Now this being the best *she* could do, it was a sign she was a low creature. Think of it—to kick at kindness, and kneel from terror. But the sternness on the face of the wise woman came from the same heart and the same feeling as the kindness that had shone from it before. The only thing that could save the princess from her hatefulness, was that she should be made to mind somebody else than her own miserable Somebody.

Without saying a word, the wise woman reached down her hand, took one of Rosamond's, and, lifting her to her feet, led her along through the moonlight. Every now and then a gush of obstinacy would well up in the heart of the princess, and she would give a great ill-tempered tug, and pull her hand away; but then the wise woman would gaze down upon her with such a look, that she instantly sought again the hand she had rejected, in pure terror lest she should be eaten upon the spot. And so they would walk on again; and when the wind blew the folds of the cloak against the princess, she found them soft as her mother's camel-hair shawl.

After a little while the wise woman began to sing to her, and the princess could not help listening; for the soft wind amongst the low dry bushes of the heath, the rustle of their own steps, and the trailing of the wise woman's cloak, were the only sounds beside.

And this is the song she sang:—

"Out in the cold,
    With a thin-worn fold
    Of withered gold
    Around her rolled,
Hangs in the air the weary moon.
    She is old, old, old;
    And her bones all cold,
    And her tales all told,
    And her things all sold,
And she has no breath to croon.

    Like a castaway clout,
    She is quite shut out!
    She might call and shout,
    But no one about

Would ever call back, 'Who's there?'
  There is never a hut,
  Not a door to shut,
  Not a footpath or rut,
  Long road or short cut,
Leading to anywhere!

  She is all alone
  Like a dog-picked bone,
  The poor old crone!
  She fain would groan,
But she cannot find the breath.
  She once had a fire;
  But she built it no higher,
  And only sat nigher
  Till she saw it expire;
And now she is cold as death.

  She never will smile
  All the lonesome while.
  Oh the mile after mile,
  And never a stile!
And never a tree or a stone!
  She has not a tear:
  Afar and anear
  It is all so drear,
  But she does not care,
Her heart is as dry as a bone.

  None to come near her!
  No one to cheer her!
  No one to jeer her!
  No one to hear her!
Not a thing to lift and hold!
  She is always awake,
  But her heart will not break:
  She can only quake,
  Shiver, and shake:
The old woman is very cold."

As strange as the song, was the crooning wailing
tune that the wise woman sung. At the first note
almost, you would have thought she wanted to
frighten the princess; and so indeed she did. For
when people *will* be naughty, they have to be frightened, and they are not expected to like it. The
princess grew angry, pulled her hand away, and
cried,—

"*You* are the ugly old woman. I hate you!"

Therewith she stood still, expecting the wise
woman to stop also, perhaps coax her to go on: if she
did, she was determined not to move a step. But the
wise woman never even looked about: she kept
walking on steadily, the same space as before. Little
Obstinate thought for certain she would turn; for she
regarded herself as much too precious to be left behind. But on and on the wise woman went, until she
had vanished away in the dim moonlight. Then all
at once the princess perceived that she was left alone
with the moon, looking down on her from the height
of her loneliness. She was horribly frightened, and
began to run after the wise woman, calling aloud.
But the song she had just heard came back to the
sound of her own running feet,—

> All all alone,
> Like a dog-picked bone!

and again,—

> She might call and shout,
> And no one about
> Would ever call back, "Who's there?"

and she screamed as she ran. How she wished she
knew the old woman's name, that she might call it
after her through the moonlight!

But the wise woman had, in truth, heard the first

sound of her running feet, and stopped and turned, waiting. What with running and crying, however, and a fall or two as she ran, the princess never saw her until she fell right into her arms—and the same moment into a fresh rage; for as soon as any trouble was over the princess was always ready to begin another. The wise woman therefore pushed her away, and walked on; while the princess ran scolding and storming after her. She had to run till, from very fatigue, her rudeness ceased. Her heart gave way; she burst into tears, and ran on silently weeping.

A minute more and the wise woman stooped, and lifting her in her arms, folded her cloak around her. Instantly she fell asleep, and slept as soft and as soundly as if she had been in her own bed. She slept till the moon went down; she slept till the sun rose up; she slept till he climbed the topmost sky; she slept till he went down again, and the poor old moon came peaking and peering out once more: and all that time the wise woman went walking on and on very fast. And now they had reached a spot where a few fir-trees came to meet them through the moonlight.

At the same time the princess awaked, and popping her head out between the folds of the wise woman's cloak—a very ugly little owlet she looked —saw that they were entering the wood. Now there is something awful about every wood, especially in the moonlight; and perhaps a fir-wood is more awful than other woods. For one thing, it lets a little more light through, rendering the darkness a little more visible, as it were; and then the trees go stretching away up towards the moon, and look as if they cared nothing about the creatures below them— not like the broad trees with soft wide leaves that, in the darkness even, look sheltering. So the princess is not to be blamed that she was very much frightened. She is hardly to be blamed either that, assured

the wise woman was an ogress carrying her to her
castle to eat her up, she began again to kick and
scream violently, as those of my readers who are of
the same sort as herself will consider the right and
natural thing to do. The wrong in her was this—
that she had led such a bad life, that she did not
know a good woman when she saw her; took her for
one like herself, even after she had slept in her arms.

Immediately the wise woman set her down, and,
walking on, within a few paces vanished among the
trees. Then the cries of the princess rent the air, but
the fir-trees never heeded her; not one of their hard
little needles gave a single shiver for all the noise
she made. But there were creatures in the forest who
were soon quite as much interested in her cries as
the fir-trees were indifferent to them. They began to
hearken and howl and snuff about, and run hither
and thither, and grin with their white teeth, and
light up the green lamps in their eyes. In a minute or
two a whole army of wolves and hyenas were rushing from all quarters through the pillar-like stems
of the fir-trees, to the place where she stood calling
them, without knowing it. The noise she made herself, however, prevented her from hearing either
their howls or the soft pattering of their many
trampling feet as they bounded over the fallen fir
needles and cones.

One huge old wolf had outsped the rest—not that
he could run faster, but that from experience he
could more exactly judge whence the cries came,
and as he shot through the wood, she caught sight at
last of his lamping eyes coming swiftly nearer and
nearer. Terror silenced her. She stood with her
mouth open, as if she were going to eat the wolf, but
she had no breath to scream with, and her tongue
curled up in her mouth like a withered and frozen
leaf. She could do nothing but stare at the coming
monster. And now he was taking a few shorter

bounds, measuring the distance for the one final leap that should bring him upon her, when out stepped the wise woman from behind the very tree by which she had set the princess down, caught the wolf by the throat half-way in his last spring, shook him once, and threw him from her dead. Then she turned towards the princess, who flung herself into her arms, and was instantly lapped in the folds of her cloak.

But now the huge army of wolves and hyenas had rushed like a sea around them, whose waves leaped with hoarse roar and hollow yell up against the wise woman. But she, like a strong stately vessel, moved unhurt through the midst of them. Ever as they leaped against her cloak, they dropped and slunk away back through the crowd. Others ever succeeded, and ever in their turn fell, and drew back confounded. For some time she walked on attended and assailed on all sides by the howling pack. Suddenly they turned and swept away, vanishing in the depths of the forest. She neither slackened nor hastened her step, but went walking on as before.

In a little while she unfolded her cloak, and let the princess look out. The firs had ceased; and they were on a lofty height of moorland, stony and bare and dry, with tufts of heather and a few small plants here and there. About the heath, on every side, lay the forest, looking in the moonlight like a cloud; and above the forest, like the shaven crown of a monk, rose the bare moor over which they were walking. Presently, a little way in front of them, the princess espied a whitewashed cottage, gleaming in the moon. As they came nearer, she saw that the roof was covered with thatch, over which the moss had grown green. It was a very simple, humble place, not in the least terrible to look at, and yet, as soon as she saw it, her fear again awoke, and always, as soon as her fear awoke, the trust of the princess fell into a dead sleep. Foolish and useless as she might by this time have known it, she once more began kicking and screaming, whereupon, yet once more, the wise woman set her down on the heath, a few yards from the back of the cottage, and saying only, "No one ever gets into my house who does not knock at the door, and ask to come in," disappeared round the corner of the cottage, leaving the princess alone with the moon—two white faces in the cone of the night.

III

The moon stared at the princess, and the princess stared at the moon; but the moon had the best of it, and the princess began to cry. And now the question was between the moon and the cottage. The princess thought she knew the worst of the moon, and she knew nothing at all about the cottage, therefore she would stay with the moon. Strange, was it not, that she should have been so long with the wise woman, and yet know *nothing* about that cottage? As for the moon, she did not by any means know the worst of her, or even, that, if she were to fall asleep where she could find her, the old witch would certainly do her best to twist her face.

But she had scarcely sat a moment longer before she was assailed by all sorts of fresh fears. First of all, the soft wind blowing gently through the dry stalks of the heather and its thousands of little bells raised a sweet rustling, which the princess took for the hissing of serpents, for you know she had been naughty for so long that she could not in a great many things tell the good from the bad. Then nobody could deny that there, all round about the heath, like a ring of darkness, lay the gloomy firwood, and the princess knew what it was full of, and every now and then she thought she heard the howling of its wolves and hyenas. And who could tell but some of them might break from their covert and sweep like a shadow across the heath? Indeed, it was not once nor twice that for a moment she was fully persuaded she saw a great beast coming leaping and bounding through the moonlight to have her all to himself. She did not know that not a single evil creature dared set foot on that heath, or that, if one should do so, it would that instant wither up and cease. If an army of them had rushed to invade it, it would have melted away on the edge of it, and ceased like a dying wave.—She even imagined that the moon was slowly coming nearer and nearer down the sky to take her and freeze her to death in her arms. The wise woman, too, she felt sure, although her cottage looked asleep, was watching her at some little window. In this, however, she would have been quite right, if she had only imagined enough—namely, that the wise woman was watching *over* her from the little window. But after all, somehow, the thought of the wise woman was less frightful than that of any of her other terrors, and at length she began to wonder whether it might not turn out that she was no ogress, but only a rude, ill-bred, tyrannical, yet on the whole not altogether ill-meaning person. Hardly had the possibility arisen in her mind, before she was on her feet: if the woman was any thing short of an ogress, her cottage must be better than that horrible loneliness, with nothing in all the world but a stare; and even an ogress had at least the shape and look of a human being.

She darted round the end of the cottage to find the front. But, to her surprise, she came only to another back, for no door was to be seen. She tried the farther end, but still no door. She must have passed it as she ran—but no—neither in gable nor in side was any to be found.

A cottage without a door!—she rushed at it in a rage and kicked at the wall with her feet. But the wall was hard as iron, and hurt her sadly through her gay silken slippers. She threw herself on the heath, which came up to the walls of the cottage on every side, and roared and screamed with rage. Suddenly,

however, she remembered how her screaming had
brought the horde of wolves and hyenas about her
in the forest, and, ceasing at once, lay still, gazing
yet again at the moon. And then came the thought
of her parents in the palace at home. In her mind's
eye she saw her mother sitting at her embroidery
with the tears dropping upon it, and her father staring into the fire as if he were looking for her in its
glowing caverns. It is true that if they had both
been in tears by her side because of her naughtiness, she would not have cared a straw; but now
her own forlorn condition somehow helped her to
understand their grief at having lost her, and not
only a great longing to be back in her comfortable
home, but a feeble flutter of genuine love for her
parents awoke in her heart as well, and she burst into
real tears—soft, mournful tears—very different from
those of rage and disappointment to which she was
so much used. And another very remarkable thing
was that the moment she began to love her father
and mother, she began to wish to see the wise
woman again. The idea of her being an ogress
vanished utterly, and she thought of her only as one
to take her in from the moon, and the loneliness, and
the terrors of the forest-haunted heath, and hide her
in a cottage with not even a door for the horrid
wolves to howl against.

But the old woman—as the princess called her,
not knowing that her real name was the Wise
Woman—had told her that she must knock at the
door: how was she to do that when there was no
door? But again she bethought herself—that, if she
could not do all she was told, she could, at least, do
a part of it: if she could not knock at the door, she
could at least knock—say on the wall, for there was
nothing else to knock upon—and perhaps the old
woman would hear her, and lift her in by some
window. Thereupon, she rose at once to her feet,

and picking up a stone, began to knock on the wall with it. A loud noise was the result, and she found she was knocking on the very door itself. For a moment she feared the old woman would be offended, but the next, there came a voice, saying,

"Who is there?"

The princess answered,

"Please, old woman, I did not mean to knock so loud."

To this there came no reply.

Then the princess knocked again, this time with her knuckles, and the voice came again, saying,

"Who is there?"

And the princess answered,

"Rosamond."

Then a second time there was silence. But the princess soon ventured to knock a third time.

"What do you want?" said the voice.

"Oh, please, let me in!" said the princess. "The moon will keep staring at me; and I hear the wolves in the wood."

Then the door opened, and the princess entered. She looked all around, but saw nothing of the wise woman.

It was a single bare little room, with a white deal table, and a few old wooden chairs, a fire of fir-wood on the hearth, the smoke of which smelt sweet, and a patch of thick-growing heath in one corner. Poor as it was, compared to the grand place Rosamond had left, she felt no little satisfaction as she shut the door, and looked around her. And what with the sufferings and terrors she had left outside, the new kind of tears she had shed, the love she had begun to feel for her parents, and the trust she had begun to place in the wise woman, it seemed to her as if her soul had grown larger of a sudden, and she had left the days of her childishness and naughtiness far behind her. People are so ready to think themselves changed when it is only their mood that is changed! Those who are good-tempered because it is a fine day, will be ill-tempered when it rains: their selves are just the same both days; only in the one case, the fine weather has got into them, in the other the rainy. Rosamond, as she sat warming herself by the glow of the peat-fire, turning over in her mind all that had passed, and feeling how pleasant the change in her feelings was, began by degrees to think how very good she had grown, and how very good she was to have grown good, and how extremely good she must always have been that she was able to grow so very good as she now felt she had grown; and she became so absorbed in her self-admiration as never to notice either that the fire was dying, or that a heap of fir-cones lay in a corner near it. Suddenly, a great wind came roaring down the chimney, and scattered the ashes about the floor; a tremendous rain followed, and fell hissing on the embers; the moon was swallowed up, and there was darkness all about her. Then a flash of lightning, followed by a peal of thunder, so terrified the princess, that she cried aloud for the old woman, but there came no answer to her cry.

Then in her terror the princess grew angry, and saying to herself, "She must be somewhere in the place, else who was there to open the door to me?" began to shout and yell, and call the wise woman all the bad names she had been in the habit of throwing at her nurses. But there came not a single sound in reply.

Strange to say, the princess never thought of telling herself now how naughty she was, though that would surely have been reasonable. On the contrary, she thought she had a perfect right to be angry, for was she not most desperately ill used—and a princess too? But the wind howled on, and the rain kept pouring down the chimney, and every now and then the lightning burst out, and the thunder rushed after it, as if the great lumbering sound could ever think to catch up with the swift light!

At length the princess had again grown so angry, frightened, and miserable, all together, that she jumped up and hurried about the cottage with out-stretched arms, trying to find the wise woman. But being in a bad temper always makes people stupid, and presently she struck her forehead such a blow against something—she thought herself it felt like the old woman's cloak—that she fell back—not on the floor, though, but on the patch of heather, which felt as soft and pleasant as any bed in the palace. There, worn out with weeping and rage, she soon fell fast asleep.

She dreamed that she was the old cold woman up in the sky, with no home and no friends, and no nothing at all, not even a pocket; wandering, wandering forever, over a desert of blue sand, never to get to anywhere, and never to lie down or die. It was no use stopping to look about her, for what had she to do but forever look about her as she went on and on and on—never seeing any thing, and never expecting to see any thing! The only shadow of a hope she had was, that she might by slow degrees grow thinner and thinner, until at last she wore away to nothing at all; only alas! she could not detect the least sign that she had yet begun to grow thinner. The hopelessness grew at length so unendurable that she woke with a start. Seeing the face of the wise woman bending over her, she threw her arms around her neck and held up her mouth to be kissed. And the kiss of the wise woman was like the rose-gardens of Damascus.

IV

The wise woman lifted her tenderly, and washed and dressed her far more carefully than even her nurse. Then she set her down by the fire, and prepared her breakfast. The princess was very hungry, and the bread and milk as good as it could be, so that she thought she had never in her life eaten any thing nicer. Nevertheless, as soon as she began to have enough, she said to herself,—

"Ha! I see how it is! The old woman wants to fatten me! That is why she gives me such nice creamy milk. She doesn't kill me now because she's going to kill me then! She *is* an ogress, after all!"

Thereupon she laid down her spoon, and would not eat another mouthful—only followed the basin with longing looks, as the wise woman carried it away.

When she stopped eating, her hostess knew exactly what she was thinking; but it was one thing to understand the princess, and quite another to make the princess understand her: that would require time. For the present she took no notice, but went about the affairs of the house, sweeping the floor, brushing down the cobwebs, cleaning the hearth, dusting the table and chairs, and watering the bed to keep it fresh and alive—for she never had more than one guest at a time, and never would allow that guest to go to sleep upon any thing that had no life in it. All the time she was thus busied, she spoke not a word to the princess, which, with the princess, went to confirm her notion of her purposes. But whatever she might have said would have been only perverted by the princess into yet stronger proof of her evil designs, for a fancy in her own head would outweigh any multitude of facts in another's. She kept staring at the fire, and never looked round to see what the wise woman might be doing.

By and by she came close up to the back of her chair, and said,

"Rosamond!"

But the princess had fallen into one of her sulky moods, and shut herself up with her own ugly Somebody; so she never looked round or even answered the wise woman.

"Rosamond," she repeated, "I am going out. If you are a good girl, that is, if you do as I tell you, I will carry you back to your father and mother the moment I return."

The princess did not take the least notice.

"Look at me, Rosamond," said the wise woman.

But Rosamond never moved—never even shrugged her shoulders—perhaps because they were already up to her ears, and could go no farther.

"I want to help you to do what I tell you," said the wise woman. "Look at me."

Still Rosamond was motionless and silent, saying only to herself,

"I know what she's after! She wants to show me her horrid teeth. But I won't look. I'm not going to be frightened out of my senses to please her."

"You had better look, Rosamond. Have you forgotten how you kissed me this morning?"

But Rosamond now regarded that little throb of affection as a momentary weakness into which the deceitful ogress had betrayed her, and almost despised herself for it. She was one of those who the more they are coaxed are the more disagreeable. For such, the wise woman had an awful punishment, but she remembered that the princess had been very ill brought up, and therefore wished to try her with all gentleness first.

She stood silent for a moment, to see what effect her words might have. But Rosamond only said to herself,—

"She wants to fatten and eat me."

And it was such a little while since she had looked into the wise woman's loving eyes, thrown her arms round her neck, and kissed her!

"Well," said the wise woman gently, after pausing as long as it seemed possible she might bethink herself, "I must tell you then without; only whoever listens with her back turned, listens but half, and gets but half the help."

"She wants to fatten me," said the princess.

"You must keep the cottage tidy while I am out. When I come back, I must see the fire bright, the hearth swept, and the kettle boiling; no dust on the table or chairs, the windows clear, the floor clean, and the heather in blossom—which last comes of sprinkling it with water three times a day. When you are hungry, put your hand into that hole in the wall, and you will find a meal."

"She wants to fatten me," said the princess.

"But on no account leave the house till I come back," continued the wise woman, "or you will grievously repent it. Remember what you have already gone through to reach it. Dangers lie all around this cottage of mine; but inside, it is the safest place—in fact the only quite safe place in all the country."

"She means to eat me," said the princess, "and therefore wants to frighten me from running away."

She heard the voice no more. Then, suddenly startled at the thought of being alone, she looked hastily over her shoulder. The cottage was indeed empty of all visible life. It was soundless, too: there was not even a ticking clock or a flapping flame.

The fire burned still and smouldering-wise; but it was all the company she had, and she turned again to stare into it.

Soon she began to grow weary of having nothing to do. Then she remembered that the old woman, as she called her, had told her to keep the house tidy.

"The miserable little pig-sty!" she said. "Where's the use of keeping such a hovel clean!"

But in truth she would have been glad of the employment, only just because she had been told to do it, she was unwilling; for there *are* people—however unlikely it may seem—who object to doing a thing for no other reason than that it is required of them.

"I am a princess," she said, "and it is very improper to ask me to do such a thing."

She might have judged it quite as suitable for a princess to sweep away the dust as to sit the centre of a world of dirt. But just because she ought, she wouldn't. Perhaps she feared that if she gave in to doing her duty once, she might have to do it always—which was true enough—for that was the very thing for which she had been specially born.

Unable, however, to feel quite comfortable in the resolve to neglect it, she said to herself, "I'm sure there's time enough for such a nasty job as that!" and sat on, watching the fire as it burned away, the glowing red casting off white flakes, and sinking lower and lower on the hearth.

By and by, merely for want of something to do, she would see what the old woman had left for her in the hole of the wall. But when she put in her hand she found nothing there, except the dust which she ought by this time to have wiped away. Never reflecting that the wise woman had told her she would find food there *when she was hungry,* she flew into one of her furies, calling her a cheat, and a thief, and a liar, and an ugly old witch, and an ogress, and I do not know how many wicked names besides. She raged until she was quite exhausted, and then fell fast asleep on her chair. When she awoke the fire was out.

By this time she was hungry; but without looking in the hole, she began again to storm at the wise woman, in which labor she would no doubt have once more exhausted herself, had not something white caught her eye: it was the corner of a napkin hanging from the hole in the wall. She bounded to it, and there was a dinner for her of something strangely good—one of her favorite dishes, only better than she had ever tasted it before. This might surely have at least changed her mood towards the wise woman; but she only grumbled to herself that it was as it ought to be, ate up the food, and lay down on the bed, never thinking of fire, or dust, or water for the heather.

The wind began to moan about the cottage, and grew louder and louder, till a great gust came down the chimney, and again scattered the white ashes all over the place. But the princess was by this time fast asleep, and never woke till the wind had sunk to silence. One of the consequences, however, of sleeping when one ought to be awake is waking when one ought to be asleep; and the princess awoke in the black midnight, and found enough to keep her awake. For although the wind had fallen, there was a far more terrible howling than that of the wildest wind all about the cottage. Nor was the howling all; the air was full of strange cries; and everywhere she heard the noise of claws scratching against the house, which seemed all doors and windows, so crowded were the sounds, and from so many directions. All the night long she lay half swooning, yet listening to the hideous noises. But with the first glimmer of morning they ceased.

Then she said to herself, "How fortunate it was that I woke! They would have eaten me up if I had been asleep." The miserable little wretch actually talked as if she had kept them out! If she had done her work in the day, she would have slept through the terrors of the darkness, and awaked fearless; whereas now, she had in the storehouse of her heart a whole harvest of agonies, reaped from the dun fields of the night!

They were neither wolves nor hyenas which had caused her such dismay, but creatures of the air, more frightful still, which, as soon as the smoke of the burning fir-wood ceased to spread itself abroad, and the sun was a sufficient distance down the sky, and the lone cold woman was out, came flying and howling about the cottage, trying to get in at every door and window. Down the chimney they would have got, but that at the heart of the fire there always lay a certain fir-cone, which looked like solid gold red-hot, and which, although it might easily get covered up with ashes, so as to be quite invisible, was continually in a glow fit to kindle all the fir-cones in the world; this it was which had kept the horrible birds—some say they have a claw at the tip of every wing-feather—from tearing the poor naughty princess to pieces, and gobbling her up.

When she rose and looked about her, she was dismayed to see what a state the cottage was in. The fire was out, and the windows were all dim with the wings and claws of the dirty birds, while the bed from which she had just risen was brown and withered, and half its purple bells had fallen. But she consoled herself that she could set all to rights in a few minutes—only she must breakfast first. And, sure enough, there was a basin of the delicious bread and milk ready for her in the hole of the wall!

After she had eaten it, she felt comfortable, and

sat for a long time building castles in the air—till she was actually hungry again, without having done an atom of work. She ate again, and was idle again, and ate again. Then it grew dark, and she went trembling to bed, for now she remembered the horrors of the last night. This time she never slept at all, but spent the long hours in grievous terror, for the noises were worse than before. She vowed she would not pass another night in such a hateful haunted old shed for all the ugly women, witches, and ogresses in the wide world. In the morning, however, she fell asleep, and slept late.

Breakfast was of course her first thought, after which she could not avoid that of work. It made her very miserable, but she feared the consequences of being found with it undone. A few minutes before noon, she actually got up, took her pinafore for a duster, and proceeded to dust the table. But the wood-ashes flew about so, that it seemed useless to attempt getting rid of them, and she sat down again to think what was to be done. But there is very little indeed to be done when we will not do that which we have to do.

Her first thought now was to run away at once while the sun was high, and get through the forest before night came on. She fancied she could easily go back the way she had come, and get home to her father's palace. But not the most experienced traveller in the world can ever go back the way the wise woman has brought him.

She got up and went to the door. It was locked! What could the old woman have meant by telling her not to leave the cottage? She was indignant.

The wise woman had meant to make it difficult, but not impossible. Before the princess, however, could find the way out, she heard a hand at the door, and darted in terror behind it. The wise woman opened it, and, leaving it open, walked straight to the hearth. Rosamond immediately slid out, ran a little way, and then laid herself down in the long heather.

V

The wise woman walked straight up to the hearth, looked at the fire, looked at the bed, glanced round the room, and went up to the table. When she saw the one streak in the thick dust which the princess had left there, a smile, half sad, half pleased, like the sun peeping through a cloud on a rainy day in spring, gleamed over her face. She went at once to the door, and called in a loud voice,

"Rosamond, come to me."

All the wolves and hyenas, fast asleep in the wood, heard her voice, and shivered in their dreams. No wonder then that the princess trembled, and found herself compelled, she could not understand how, to obey the summons. She rose, like the guilty thing she felt, forsook of herself the hiding-place she had chosen, and walked slowly back to the cottage she had left full of the signs of her shame. When she entered, she saw the wise woman on her knees, building up the fire with fir-cones. Already the flame was climbing through the heap in all directions, crackling gently, and sending a sweet aromatic odor through the dusty cottage.

"That is my part of the work," she said, rising. "Now you do yours. But first let me remind you that if you had not put it off, you would have found it not only far easier, but by and by quite pleasant work, much more pleasant than you can imagine now; nor would you have found the time go wearily: you would neither have slept in the day and let the fire out, nor waked at night and heard the howling of the beast-birds. More than all, you would have been glad to see me when I came back; and would have leaped into my arms instead of standing there, looking so ugly and foolish."

As she spoke, suddenly she held up before the princess a tiny mirror, so clear that nobody looking into it could tell what it was made of, or even see it at all—only the thing reflected in it. Rosamond saw a child with dirty fat cheeks, greedy mouth, cowardly eyes—which, not daring to look forward, seemed trying to hide behind an impertinent nose—stooping shoulders, tangled hair, tattered clothes, and smears and stains everywhere. That was what she had made herself. And to tell the truth, she was shocked at the sight, and immediately began, in her dirty heart, to lay the blame on the wise woman, because she had taken her away from her nurses and her fine clothes; while all the time she knew well enough that, close by the heather-bed, was the loveliest little well, just big enough to wash in, the water of which was always springing fresh from the ground, and running away through the wall. Beside it lay the whitest of linen towels, with a comb made of mother-of-pearl, and a brush of fir-needles, any one of which she had been far too lazy to use. She dashed the glass out of the wise woman's hand, and there it lay, broken into a thousand pieces!

Without a word, the wise woman stooped, and gathered the fragments—did not leave searching until she had gathered the last atom, and she laid them all carefully, one by one, in the fire, now blazing high on the hearth. Then she stood up and looked at the princess, who had been watching her sulkily.

"Rosamond," she said, with a countenance awful in its sternness, "until you have cleansed this room—"

"She calls it a room!" sneered the princess to herself.

"You shall have no morsel to eat. You may drink of the well, but nothing else you shall have. When the work I set you is done, you will find food in the same place as before. I am going from home again; and again I warn you not to leave the house."

"She calls it a house!—It's a good thing she's going out of it anyhow!" said the princess, turning her back for mere rudeness, for she was one who, even if she liked a thing before, would dislike it the moment any person in authority over her desired her to do it.

When she looked again, the wise woman had vanished.

Thereupon the princess ran at once to the door, and tried to open it; but open it would not. She searched on all sides, but could discover no way of getting out. The windows would not open—at least she could not open them; and the only outlet seemed the chimney, which she was afraid to try because of the fire, which looked angry, she thought, and shot out green flames when she went near it. So she sat down to consider. One may well wonder what room for consideration there was—with all her work lying undone behind her. She sat thus, however, considering, as she called it, until hunger began to sting her, when she jumped up and put her hand as usual in the hole of the wall: there was nothing there. She fell straight into one of her stupid rages; but neither her hunger nor the hole in the wall heeded her rage. Then, in a burst of self-pity, she fell a-weeping, but neither the hunger nor the hole cared for her tears. The darkness began to come on, and her hunger grew and grew, and the terror of the wild noises of the last night invaded her. Then she began to feel cold, and saw that the fire was dying. She darted to the heap of cones, and fed it. It blazed up cheerily,

and she was comforted a little. Then she thought
with herself it would surely be better to give in so
far, and do a little work, than die of hunger. So
catching up a duster, she began upon the table. The
dust flew about and nearly choked her. She ran to
the well to drink, and was refreshed and encouraged.
Perceiving now that it was a tedious plan to wipe the
dust from the table on to the floor, whence it would
have all to be swept up again, she got a wooden
platter, wiped the dust into that, carried it to the fire,
and threw it in. But all the time she was getting more
and more hungry, and, although she tried the
hole again and again, it was only to become more
and more certain that work she must if she would
eat.

At length all the furniture was dusted, and she
began to sweep the floor, which happily, she
thought of sprinkling with water, as from the window she had seen them do to the marble court of the
palace. That swept, she rushed again to the hole
but still no food! She was on the verge of another
rage, when the thought came that she might have
forgotten something. To her dismay she found that
table and chairs and every thing was again covered
with dust—not so badly as before, however. Again
she set to work, driven by hunger, and drawn by
the hope of eating, and yet again, after a second
careful wiping, sought the hole. But no! nothing was
there for her! What could it mean?

Her asking this question was a sign of progress: it
showed that she expected the wise woman to keep
her word. Then she bethought her that she had forgotten the household utensils, and the dishes and
plates, some of which wanted to be washed as well
as dusted.

Faint with hunger, she set to work yet again. One
thing made her think of another, until at length she

had cleaned every thing she could think of. Now surely she must find some food in the hole!

When this time also there was nothing, she began once more to abuse the wise woman as false and treacherous;—but ah! there was the bed unwatered! That was soon amended.—Still no supper! Ah! there was the hearth unswept, and the fire wanted making up!—Still no supper! What else could there be? She was at her wits' end, and in very weariness, not laziness this time, sat down and gazed into the fire. There, as she gazed, she spied something brilliant, —shining even, in the midst of the fire: it was the little mirror all whole again; but little she knew that the dust which she had thrown into the fire had helped to heal it. She drew it out carefully, and, looking into it, saw, not indeed the ugly creature she had seen there before, but still a very dirty little animal; whereupon she hurried to the well, took off her clothes, plunged into it, and washed herself clean. Then she brushed and combed her hair, made her clothes as tidy as might be, and ran to the hole in the wall: there was a huge basin of bread and milk!

Never had she eaten any thing with half the relish! Alas! however, when she had finished, she did not wash the basin, but left it as it was, revealing how entirely all the rest had been done only from hunger. Then she threw herself on the heather, and was fast asleep in a moment. Never an evil bird came near her all that night, nor had she so much as one troubled dream.

In the morning as she lay awake before getting up, she spied what seemed a door behind the tall eight-day clock that stood silent in the corner.

"Ah!" she thought, "that must be the way out!" and got up instantly. The first thing she did, however, was to go to the hole in the wall. Nothing was there.

"Well, I am hardly used!" she cried aloud. "All that cleaning for the cross old woman yesterday, and this for my trouble,—nothing for breakfast! Not even a crust of bread! Does Mistress Ogress fancy a princess will bear that?"

The poor foolish creature seemed to think that the work of one day ought to serve for the next day too! But that is nowhere the way in the whole universe. How could there be a universe in that case? And even she never dreamed of applying the same rule to her breakfast.

"How good I was all yesterday!" she said, "and how hungry and ill used I am to-day!"

But she would *not* be a slave, and do over again to-day what she had done only last night! *She* didn't care about her breakfast! She might have it no doubt if she dusted all the wretched place again, but she was not going to do that—at least, without seeing first what lay behind the clock!

Off she darted, and putting her hand behind the clock found the latch of a door. It lifted, and the door opened a little way. By squeezing hard, she managed to get behind the clock, and so through the door. But how she stared, when, instead of the open heath, she found herself on the marble floor of a large and stately room, lighted only from above. Its walls were strengthened by pilasters, and in every space between was a large picture, from cornice to floor. She did not know what to make of it. Surely she had run all round the cottage, and certainly had seen nothing of this size near it! She forgot that she had also run round what she took for a hay-mow, a peat-stack, and several other things which looked of no consequence in the moonlight.

"So, then," she cried, "the old woman *is* a cheat! I believe she's an ogress, after all, and lives in a palace—though she pretends it's only a cottage, to keep people from suspecting that she eats good little children like me!"

Had the princess been tolerably tractable, she would, by this time, have known a good deal about the wise woman's beautiful house, whereas she had never till now got farther than the porch. Neither was she at all in its innermost places now.

But, king's daughter as she was, she was not a little daunted when, stepping forward from the recess of the door, she saw what a great lordly hall it was. She dared hardly look to the other end, it seemed so far off: so she began to gaze at the things near her, and the pictures first of all, for she had a great liking for pictures. One in particular attracted her attention. She came back to it several times, and at length stood absorbed in it.

A blue summer sky, with white fleecy clouds floating beneath it, hung over a hill green to the very top, and alive with streams darting down its sides toward the valley below. On the face of the hill strayed a flock of sheep feeding, attended by a shepherd and two dogs. A little way apart, a girl stood with bare feet in a brook, building across it a bridge of rough stones. The wind was blowing her hair back from her rosy face. A lamb was feeding close beside her; and a sheepdog was trying to reach her hand to lick it.

"Oh, how I wish I were that little girl!" said the princess aloud. "I wonder how it is that some people are made to be so much happier than others! If I were that little girl, no one would ever call me naughty."

She gazed and gazed at the picture. At length she said to herself,

"I do not believe it is a picture. It is the real country, with a real hill, and a real little girl upon it. I shall soon see whether this isn't another of the old witch's cheats!"

She went close up to the picture, lifted her foot, and stepped over the frame.

"I am free, I am free!" she exclaimed; and she felt the wind upon her cheek.

The sound of a closing door struck on her ear. She turned—and there was a blank wall, without door or window, behind her. The hill with the sheep was before her, and she set out at once to reach it.

Now, if I am asked how this could be, I can only answer, that it was a result of the interaction of things outside and things inside, of the wise woman's skill, and the silly child's folly. If this does not satisfy my questioner, I can only add, that the wise woman was able to do far more wonderful things than this.

VI

Meantime the wise woman was busy as she always was; and her business now was with the child of the shepherd and shepherdess, away in the north. Her name was Agnes.

Her father and mother were poor, and could not give her many things. Rosamond would have utterly despised the rude, simple playthings she had. Yet in one respect they were of more value far than hers: the king bought Rosamond's with his money; Agnes's father made hers with his hands.

And while Agnes had but few things—not seeing many things about her, and not even knowing that there were many things anywhere, she did not wish for many things, and was therefore neither covetous nor avaricious.

She played with the toys her father made her, and thought them the most wonderful things in the world—windmills, and little crooks, and waterwheels, and sometimes lambs made all of wool, and dolls made out of the leg-bones of sheep, which her mother dressed for her; and of such playthings she was never tired. Sometimes, however, she preferred playing with stones, which were plentiful, and flowers, which were few, or the brooks that ran down the hill, of which, although they were many, she could only play with one at a time, and that, indeed, troubled her a little—or live lambs that were not all wool, or the sheep-dogs, which were very friendly with her, and the best of playfellows, as she thought, for she had no human ones to compare them with.

Neither was she greedy after nice things, but content, as well she might be, with the homely food provided for her. Nor was she by nature particularly self-willed or disobedient; she generally did what her father and mother wished, and believed what they told her. But by degrees they had spoiled her; and this was the way: they were so proud of her that they always repeated every thing she said, and told every thing she did, even when she was present; and so full of admiration of their child were they, that they wondered and laughed at and praised things in her which in another child would never have struck them as the least remarkable, and some things even which would in another have disgusted them altogether. Impertinent and rude things done by *their* child they thought *so* clever! laughing at them as something quite marvellous; her commonplace speeches were said over again as if they had been the finest poetry; and the pretty ways which every moderately good child has were extolled as if the result of her excellent taste, and the choice of her judgment and will. They would even say sometimes that she ought not to hear her own praises for fear it should make her vain, and then whisper them behind their hands, but so loud that she could not fail to hear every word. The consequence was that she soon came to believe—so soon, that she could not recall the time when she did not believe, as the most absolute fact in the universe, that she was SOMEBODY; that is, she became most immoderately conceited.

Now as the least atom of conceit is a thing to be ashamed of, you may fancy what she was like with such a quantity of it inside her! At first it did not show itself outside in any very active form; but the wise woman had been to the cottage, and had seen her sitting alone, with such a smile of self-satisfaction upon her face as would have been quite startling to her, if she had ever been startled at any thing; for through that smile she could see lying at the root of it the worm that made it. For some smiles are like the ruddiness of certain apples, which is owing to a centipede, or other creeping thing, coiled up at the heart of them. Only her worm had a face and shape the very image of her own; and she looked so simpering, and mawkish, and self-conscious, and silly, that she made the wise woman feel rather sick.

Not that the child was a fool. Had she been, the wise woman would have only pitied and loved her, instead of feeling sick when she looked at her. She had very fair abilities, and were she once but made humble, would be capable not only of doing a good deal in time, but of beginning at once to grow to no end. But, if she were not made humble, her growing would be to a mass of distorted shapes all huddled together; so that, although the body she now showed might grow up straight and well-shaped and comely to behold, the new body that was growing inside of it, and would come out of it when she died, would be ugly, and crooked this way and that, like an aged hawthorn that has lived hundreds of years exposed upon all sides to salt sea-winds.

As time went on, this disease of self-conceit went on too, gradually devouring the good that was in her. For there is no fault that does not bring its brothers and sisters and cousins to live with it. By degrees, from thinking herself so clever, she came to fancy that whatever seemed to her, must of course be the correct judgment, and whatever she wished, the right thing; and grew so obstinate, that at length her parents feared to thwart her in any thing, knowing well that she would never give in. But there are victories far worse than defeats; and to overcome an angel too gentle to put out all his strength, and ride away in triumph on the back of a devil, is one of the poorest.

So long as she was left to take her own way and do as she would, she gave her parents little trouble. She would play about by herself in the little garden with its few hardy flowers, or amongst the heather where the bees were busy; or she would wander away amongst the hills, and be nobody knew where, sometimes from morning to night; nor did her parents venture to find fault with her.

She never went into rages like the princess, and would have thought Rosamond—oh, so ugly and vile! if she had seen her in one of her passions. But she was no better, for all that, and was quite as ugly in the eyes of the wise woman, who could not only see but read her face. What is there to choose between a face distorted to hideousness by anger, and one distorted to silliness by self-complacency? True, there is more hope of helping the angry child out of her form of selfishness than the conceited child out of hers; but on the other hand, the conceited child was not so terrible or dangerous as the wrathful one. The conceited one, however, was sometimes very angry, and then her anger was more spiteful than the other's; and, again, the wrathful one was often very conceited too. So that, on the whole, of two very unpleasant creatures, I would say that the king's daughter would have been the worse, had not the shepherd's been quite as bad.

But, as I have said, the wise woman had her eye upon her: she saw that something special must be done, else she would be one of those who kneel to their own shadows till feet grow on their knees; then go down on their hands till their hands grow into feet; then lay their faces on the ground till they grow into snouts; when at last they are a hideous sort of lizards, each of which believes himself the best, wisest, and loveliest being in the world, yea, the very centre of the universe. And so they run about forever looking for their own shadows, that they may worship them, and miserable because they cannot find them, being themselves too near the ground to have any shadows; and what becomes of them at last there is but one who knows.

The wise woman, therefore, one day walked up to the door of the shepherd's cottage, dressed like a poor woman, and asked for a drink of water. The shepherd's wife looked at her, liked her, and brought her a cup of milk. The wise woman took it, for she made it a rule to accept every kindness that was offered her.

Agnes was not by nature a greedy girl, as I have said; but self-conceit will go far to generate every other vice under the sun. Vanity, which is a form of self-conceit, has repeatedly shown itself as the deepest feeling in the heart of a horrible murderess.

That morning, at breakfast, her mother had stinted her in milk—just a little—that she might have enough to make some milk-porridge for their dinner. Agnes did not mind it at the time, but when she saw the milk now given to a beggar, as she called the wise woman—though, surely, one might ask a draught of water, and accept a draught of milk, without being a beggar in any such sense as Agnes's contemptuous use of the word implied—a cloud came upon her forehead, and a double vertical wrinkle settled over her nose. The wise woman saw it, for all her business was with Agnes though she little knew it, and, rising, went and offered the cup to the child, where she sat with her knitting in a corner. Agnes looked at it, did not want it, was inclined to refuse it from a beggar, but thinking it would show her consequence to assert her rights, took it and drank it up. For whoever is possessed by a devil, judges with the mind of that devil; and hence Agnes was guilty of such a meanness as many who are themselves capable of something just as bad will consider incredible.

The wise woman waited till she had finished it—then, looking into the empty cup, said:

"You might have given me back as much as you had no claim upon!"

Agnes turned away and made no answer—far less from shame than indignation.

The wise woman looked at the mother.

"You should not have offered it to her if you did not mean her to have it," said the mother, siding with the devil in her child against the wise woman and her child too. Some foolish people think they take another's part when they take the part he takes.

The wise woman said nothing, but fixed her eyes upon her, and soon the mother hid her face in her apron weeping. Then she turned again to Agnes, who had never looked round but sat with her back to both, and suddenly lapped her in the folds of her cloak. When the mother again lifted her eyes, she had vanished.

Never supposing she had carried away her child, but uncomfortable because of what she had said to the poor woman, the mother went to the door, and called after her as she toiled slowly up the hill. But she never turned her head; and the mother went back into her cottage.

The wise woman walked close past the shepherd and his dogs, and through the midst of his flock of sheep. The shepherd wondered where she could be going—right up the hill. There was something strange about her too, he thought; and he followed her with his eyes as she went up and up.

It was near sunset, and as the sun went down, a gray cloud settled on the top of the mountain, which his last rays turned into a rosy gold. Straight into this cloud the shepherd saw the woman hold her pace, and in it she vanished. He little imagined that his child was under her cloak.

He went home as usual in the evening, but Agnes

had not come in. They were accustomed to such an absence now and then, and were not at first frightened; but when it grew dark and she did not appear, the husband set out with his dogs in one direction, and the wife in another, to seek their child. Morning came and they had not found her. Then the whole country-side arose to search for the missing Agnes; but day after day and night after night passed, and nothing was discovered of or concerning her, until at length all gave up the search in despair except the mother, although she was nearly convinced now that the poor woman had carried her off.

One day she had wandered some distance from her cottage, thinking she might come upon the remains of her daughter at the foot of some cliff, when she came suddenly, instead, upon a disconsolate-looking creature sitting on a stone by the side of a stream. Her hair hung in tangles from her head; her clothes were tattered, and through the rents her skin showed in many places; her cheeks were white, and worn thin with hunger; the hollows were dark under her eyes, and they stood out scared and wild. When she caught sight of the shepherdess, she jumped to her feet, and would have run away, but fell down in a faint.

At first sight the mother had taken her for her own child, but now she saw, with a pang of disappointment, that she had mistaken. Full of compassion, nevertheless, she said to herself:

"If she is not my Agnes, she is as much in need of help as if she were. If I cannot be good to my own, I will be as good as I can to some other woman's; and though I should scorn to be consoled for the loss of one by the presence of another, I yet may find some gladness in rescuing one child from the death which has taken the other."

Perhaps her words were not just like these, but

her thoughts were. She took up the child, and carried her home. And this is how Rosamond came to occupy the place of the little girl whom she had envied in the picture.

VII

Notwithstanding the differences between the two girls, which were, indeed, so many that most people would have said they were not in the least alike, they were the same in this, that each cared more for her own fancies and desires than for any thing else in the world. But I will tell you another difference: the princess was like several children in one—such was the variety of her moods; and in one mood she had no recollection or care about any thing whatever belonging to a previous mood—not even if it had left her but a moment before, and had been so violent as to make her ready to put her hand in the fire to get what she wanted. Plainly she was the mere puppet of her moods, and more than that, any cunning nurse who knew her well enough could call or send away those moods almost as she pleased, like a showman pulling strings behind a show. Agnes, on the contrary, seldom changed her mood, but kept that of calm assured self-satisfaction. Father nor mother had ever by wise punishment helped her to gain a victory over herself, and do what she did not like or choose; and their folly in reasoning with one unreasonable had fixed her in her conceit. She would actually nod her head to herself in complacent pride that she had stood out against them. This, however, was not so difficult as to justify even the pride of having conquered, seeing she loved them so little, and paid so little attention to the arguments and persuasions they used. Neither, when she found herself wrapped in the dark folds of the wise woman's cloak, did she behave in the least like the princess, for she was not afraid. "She'll soon set me down," she said, too self-important to suppose that any one would dare do her an injury.

Whether it be a good thing or a bad not to be afraid depends on what the fearlessness is founded upon. Some have no fear, because they have no knowledge of the danger: there is nothing fine in that. Some are too stupid to be afraid: there is nothing fine in that. Some who are not easily frightened would yet turn their backs and run, the moment they were frightened: such never had more courage than fear. But the man who will do his work in spite of his fear is a man of true courage. The fearlessness of Agnes was only ignorance: she did not know what it was to be hurt; she had never read a single story of giant, or ogress, or wolf; and her mother had never carried out one of her threats of punishment. If the wise woman had but pinched her, she would have shown herself an abject little coward, trembling with fear at every change of motion so long as she carried her.

Nothing such, however, was in the wise woman's plan for the curing of her. On and on she carried her without a word. She knew that if she set her down she would never run after her like the princess, at least not before the evil thing was already upon her. On and on she went, never halting, never letting the light look in, or Agnes look out. She walked very fast, and got home to her cottage very soon after the princess had gone from it.

But she did not set Agnes down either in the cottage or in the great hall. She had other places, none of them alike. The place she had chosen for Agnes was a strange one—such a one as is to be found nowhere else in the wide world.

It was a great hollow sphere, made of a substance similar to that of the mirror which Rosamond had broken, but differently compounded. That substance no one could see by itself. It had neither door, nor window, nor any opening to break its perfect roundness.

The wise woman carried Agnes into a dark room, there undressed her, took from her hand her knitting-needles, and put her, naked as she was born, into the hollow sphere.

What sort of a place it was she could not tell. She could see nothing but a faint cold bluish light all about her. She could not feel that any thing supported her, and yet she did not sink. She stood for a while, perfectly calm, then sat down. Nothing bad could happen to *her*—she was so important! And, indeed, it was but this: she had cared only for Somebody, and now she was going to have only Somebody. Her own choice was going to be carried a good deal farther for her than she would have knowingly carried it for herself.

After sitting a while, she wished she had something to do, but nothing came. A little longer, and it grew wearisome. She would see whether she could not walk out of the strange luminous dusk that surrounded her.

Walk she found she could, well enough, but walk out she could not. On and on she went, keeping as much in a straight line as she might, but after walking until she was thoroughly tired, she found herself no nearer out of her prison than before. She had not, indeed, advanced a single step; for, in whatever direction she tried to go, the sphere turned round and round, answering her feet accordingly. Like a squirrel in his cage she but kept placing another spot of the cunningly-suspended sphere under her feet, and she would have been still only at its lowest point after walking for ages.

At length she cried aloud; but there was no answer. It grew dreary and drearier—in her, that is:

outside there was no change. Nothing was overhead, nothing under foot, nothing on either hand, but the same pale, faint, bluish glimmer. She wept at last, then grew very angry, and then sullen; but nobody heeded whether she cried or laughed. It was all the same to the cold unmoving twilight that rounded her. On and on went the dreary hours—or did they go at all?—"no change, no pause, no hope;"—on and on till she *felt* she was forgotten, and then she grew strangely still and fell asleep.

The moment she was asleep, the wise woman came, lifted her out, and laid her in her bosom; fed her with a wonderful milk, which she received without knowing it; nursed her all the night long, and, just ere she woke, laid her back in the blue sphere again.

When first she came to herself, she thought the horrors of the preceding day had been all a dream of the night. But they soon assserted themselves as facts, for here they were!—nothing to see but a cold blue light, and nothing to do but see it. Oh, how slowly the hours went by! She lost all notion of time. If she had been told that she had been there twenty years, she would have believed it—or twenty minutes—it would have been all the same: except for weariness, time was for her no more.

Another night came, and another still, during both of which the wise woman nursed and fed her. But she knew nothing of that, and the same one dreary day seemed ever brooding over her.

All at once, on the third day, she was aware that a naked child was seated beside her. But there was something about the child that made her shudder. She never looked at Agnes, but sat with her chin sunk on her chest, and her eyes staring at her own toes. She was the color of pale earth, with a pinched nose, and a mere slit in her face for a mouth.

"How ugly she is!" thought Agnes. "What business has she beside me!"

But it was so lonely that she would have been glad to play with a serpent, and put out her hand to touch her. She touched nothing. The child, also, put out her hand—but in the direction away from Agnes. And that was well, for if she had touched Agnes it would have killed her. Then Agnes said, "Who are you?" And the little girl said, "Who are you?" "I am Agnes," said Agnes; and the little girl said, "I am Agnes." Then Agnes thought she was mocking her, and said, "You are ugly;" and the little girl said, "You are ugly."

Then Agnes lost her temper, and put out her hands to seize the little girl; but lo! the little girl was gone, and she found herself tugging at her own hair. She let go; and there was the little girl again! Agnes was furious now, and flew at her to bite her. But she found her teeth in her own arm, and the little girl was gone—only to return again; and each time she came back she was tenfold uglier than before. And now Agnes hated her with her whole heart.

The moment she hated her, it flashed upon her with a sickening disgust that the child was not another, but her Self, her Somebody, and that she was now shut up with her for ever and ever—no more for one moment ever to be alone. In her agony of despair, sleep descended, and she slept.

When she woke, there was the little girl, heedless, ugly, miserable, staring at her own toes. All at once, the creature began to smile, but with such an odious, self-satisfied expression, that Agnes felt ashamed of seeing her. Then she began to pat her own cheeks, to stroke her own body, and examine her finger-ends, nodding her head with satisfaction. Agnes felt that there could not be such another hateful, ape-like creature, and at the same time was perfectly aware she was only doing outside of her what she herself had been doing, as long as she could remember, inside of her.

She turned sick at herself, and would gladly have been put out of existence, but for three days the odious companionship went on. By the third day, Agnes was not merely sick but ashamed of the life she had hitherto led, was despicable in her own eyes, and astonished that she had never seen the truth concerning herself before.

The next morning she woke in the arms of the wise woman; the horror had vanished from her sight, and two heavenly eyes were gazing upon her. She wept and clung to her, and the more she clung, the more tenderly did the great strong arms close around her.

When she had lain thus for a while, the wise woman carried her into her cottage, and washed her in the little well; then dressed her in clean garments, and gave her bread and milk. When she had eaten it, she called her to her, and said very solemnly,—

"Agnes, you must not imagine you are cured. That you are ashamed of yourself now is no sign that the cause for such shame has ceased. In new circumstances, especially after you have done well for a while, you will be in danger of thinking just as much of yourself as before. So beware of yourself. I am going from home, and leave you in charge of the house. Do just as I tell you till my return."

She then gave her the same directions she had formerly given Rosamond—with this difference, that she told her to go into the picture-hall when she pleased, showing her the entrance, against which the clock no longer stood—and went away, closing the door behind her.

VIII

As soon as she was left alone, Agnes set to work tidying and dusting the cottage, made up the fire, watered the bed, and cleaned the inside of the windows: the wise woman herself always kept the outside of them clean. When she had done, she found her dinner—of the same sort she was used to at home, but better—in the hole of the wall. When she had eaten it, she went to look at the pictures.

By this time her old disposition had begun to rouse again. She had been doing her duty, and had in consequence begun again to think herself Somebody. However strange it may well seem, to do one's duty will make any one conceited who only does it sometimes. Those who do it always would as soon think of being conceited of eating their dinner as of doing their duty. What honest boy would pride himself on not picking pockets? A thief who was trying to reform would. To be conceited of doing one's duty is then a sign of how little one does it, and how little one sees what a contemptible thing it is not to do it. Could any but a low creature be conceited of not being contemptible? Until our duty becomes to us common as breathing, we are poor creatures.

So Agnes began to stroke herself once more, forgetting her late self-stroking companion, and never reflecting that she was now doing what she had then abhorred. And in this mood she went into the picture-gallery.

The first picture she saw represented a square in

a great city, one side of which was occupied by a splendid marble palace, with great flights of broad steps leading up to the door. Between it and the square was a marble-paved court, with gates of brass, at which stood sentries in gorgeous uniforms, and to which was affixed the following proclamation in letters of gold, large enough for Agnes to read:—

By the will of the King, from this time until further notice, every stray child found in the realm shall be brought without a moment's delay to the palace. Whoever shall be found having done otherwise shall straightway lose his head by the hand of the public executioner.

Agnes's heart beat loud, and her face flushed.

"Can there be such a city in the world?" she said to herself. "If I only knew where it was, I should set out for it at once. *There* would be the place for a clever girl like me!"

Her eyes fell on the picture which had so enticed Rosamond. It was the very country where her father fed his flocks. Just round the shoulder of the hill was the cottage where her parents lived, where she was born and whence she had been carried by the beggar-woman.

"Ah!" she said, "they didn't know me there. They little thought what I could be, if I had the chance. If I were but in this good, kind, loving, generous king's palace, I should soon be such a great lady as they never saw! Then they would understand what a good little girl I had always been! And I shouldn't forget my poor parents like some I have read of. *I* would be generous. *I* should never be selfish and proud like girls in story-books!"

As she said this, she turned her back with disdain upon the picture of her home, and setting herself before the picture of the palace, stared at it with wide ambitious eyes, and a heart whose every beat was a throb of arrogant self-esteem.

The shepherd-child was now worse than ever the poor princess had been. For the wise woman had given her a terrible lesson one of which the princess was not capable, and she had known what it meant; yet here she was as bad as ever, therefore worse than before. The ugly creature whose presence had made her so miserable had indeed crept out of sight and mind too—but where was she? Nestling in her very heart, where most of all she had her company, and least of all could see her. The wise woman had called her out, that Agnes might see what sort of creature she was herself; but now she was snug in her soul's bed again, and she did not even suspect she was there.

After gazing a while at the palace picture, during which her ambitious pride rose and rose, she turned yet again in condescending mood, and honored the home picture with one stare more.

"What a poor, miserable spot it is compared with this lordly palace!" she said.

But presently she spied something in it she had not seen before, and drew nearer. It was the form of a little girl, building a bridge of stones over one of the hill-brooks.

"Ah, there I am myself!" she said. "That is just how I used to do.—No," she resumed, "it is not me. That snub-nosed little fright could never be meant for me! It was the frock that made me think so. But it *is* a picture of the place. I declare, I can see the smoke of the cottage rising from behind the hill! What a dull, dirty, insignificant spot it is! And what a life to lead there!"

She turned once more to the city picture. And now a strange thing took place. In proportion as the other, to the eyes of her mind, receded into the background, this, to her present bodily eyes, appeared to come forward and assume reality. At last, after it had been in this way growing upon her for some time, she gave a cry of conviction, and said aloud,—

"I do believe it is real! That frame is only a trick of the woman to make me fancy it a picture lest I should go and make my fortune. She is a witch, the ugly old creature! It would serve her right to tell the king and have her punished for not taking me to the palace—one of his poor lost children he is so fond of! I should like to see her ugly old head cut off. Anyhow I will try my luck without asking her leave. How she has ill used me!"

But at that moment, she heard the voice of the wise woman calling, "Agnes!" and, smoothing her face, she tried to look as good as she could, and walked back into the cottage. There stood the wise woman, looking all round the place, and examining her work. She fixed her eyes upon Agnes in a way that confused her, and made her cast hers down, for she felt as if she were reading her thoughts. The wise woman, however, asked no questions, but began to talk about her work, approving of some of it, which filled her with arrogance, and showing how some of it might have been done better, which filled her with resentment. But the wise woman seemed to take no care of what she might be thinking, and went straight on with her lesson. By the time it was over, the power of reading thoughts would not have been necessary to a knowledge of what was in the mind of Agnes, for it had all come to the surface— that is up into her face, which is the surface of the mind. Ere it had time to sink down again, the wise woman caught up the little mirror, and held it before her: Agnes saw her Somebody—the very embodiment of miserable conceit and ugly ill-temper. She gave such a scream of horror that the wise woman pitied her, and laying aside the mirror, took her upon her knees, and talked to her most kindly and solemnly; in particular about the necessity of destroying the ugly things that come out of the heart—so ugly that they make the very face over them ugly also.

And what was Agnes doing all the time the wise woman was talking to her? Would you believe it? —instead of thinking how to kill the ugly things in her heart, she was with all her might resolving to be more careful of her face, that is, to keep down the things in her heart so that they should not show in her face, she was resolving to be a hypocrite as well as a self-worshipper. Her heart was wormy, and the worms were eating very fast at it now.

Then the wise woman laid her gently down upon the heather-bed, and she fell fast asleep, and had an awful dream about her Somebody.

When she woke in the morning, instead of getting up to do the work of the house, she lay thinking—to evil purpose. In place of taking her dream as a warning, and thinking over what the wise woman had said the night before, she communed with herself in this fashion:—

"If I stay here longer, I shall be miserable. It is nothing better than slavery. The old witch shows me horrible things in the day to set me dreaming horrible things in the night. If I don't run away, that frightful blue prison and the disgusting girl will come back, and I shall go out of my mind. How I do wish I could find the way to the good king's palace! I shall go and look at the picture again—if it be a picture—as soon as I've got my clothes on. The work can wait. It's not my work. It's the old witch's; and she ought to do it herself."

She jumped out of bed, and hurried on her clothes. There was no wise woman to be seen; and she hastened into the hall. There was the picture, with the marble palace, and the proclamation shining in letters of gold upon its gates of brass. She stood before it, and gazed and gazed; and all the time it kept growing upon her in some strange way, until at last she was fully persuaded that it was no picture, but a real city, square, and marble palace, seen through a framed opening in the wall. She ran up to the frame, stepped over it, felt the wind blow upon her cheek, heard the sound of a closing door behind her, and was free. *Free* was she, with that creature inside her?

The same moment a terrible storm of thunder and lightning, wind and rain, came on. The uproar was appalling. Agnes threw herself upon the ground, hid her face in her hands, and there lay until it was over. As soon as she felt the sun shining on her, she rose. There was the city far away on the horizon. Without once turning to take a farewell look of the place she was leaving, she set off, as fast as her feet would carry her, in the direction of the city. So eager was she, that again and again she fell, but only to get up, and run on faster than before.

IX

The shepherdess carried Rosamond home, gave her a warm bath in the tub in which she washed her linen, made her some bread-and-milk, and after she had eaten it, put her to bed in Agnes's crib, where she slept all the rest of that day and all the following night.

When at last she opened her eyes, it was to see around her a far poorer cottage than the one she had left—very bare and uncomfortable indeed, she might well have thought; but she had come through such troubles of late, in the way of hunger and weariness and cold and fear, that she was not altogether in her ordinary mood of fault-finding, and so was able to lie enjoying the thought that at length she was safe, and going to be fed and kept warm. The idea of doing any thing in return for shelter and food and clothes, did not, however, even cross her mind.

But the shepherdess was one of that plentiful number who can be wiser concerning other women's children than concerning their own. Such will often give you very tolerable hints as to how you ought to manage your children, and will find fault neatly enough with the system you are trying to carry out; but all their wisdom goes off in talking, and there is none left for doing what they have themselves said. There is one road talk never finds, and that is the way into the talker's own hands and feet. And such never seem to know themselves —not even when they are reading about themselves

in print. Still, not being specially blinded in any
direction but their own, they can sometimes even act
with a little sense towards children who are not
theirs. They are affected with a sort of blindness
like that which renders some people incapable of
seeing, except sideways.

She came up to the bed, looked at the princess,
and saw that she was better. But she did not like
her much. There was no mark of a princess about
her, and never had been since she began to run
alone. True, hunger had brought down her fat
cheeks, but it had not turned down her impudent
nose, or driven the sullenness and greed from her
mouth. Nothing but the wise woman could do that
—and not even she, without the aid of the princess
herself. So the shepherdess thought what a poor
substitute she had got for her own lovely Agnes—
who was in fact equally repulsive, only in a way to
which she had got used; for the selfishness in her love
had blinded her to the thin pinched nose and the
mean self-satisfied mouth. It was well for the princess, though, sad as it is to say, that the shepherdess
did not take to her, for then she would most likely
have only done her harm instead of good.

"Now, my girl," she said, "you must get up, and
do something. We can't keep idle folk here."

"I'm not a folk," said Rosamond; "I'm a princess."

"A pretty princess—with a nose like that! And
all in rags too! If you tell such stories, I shall soon
let you know what I think of you."

Rosamond then understood that the mere calling
herself a princess, without having any thing to show
for it, was of no use. She obeyed and rose, for she
was hungry; but she had to sweep the floor ere she
had any thing to eat.

The shepherd came in to breakfast, and was kinder than his wife. He took her up in his arms and

would have kissed her; but she took it as an insult from a man whose hands smelt of tar, and kicked and screamed with rage. The poor man, finding he had made a mistake, set her down at once. But to look at the two, one might well have judged it condescension rather than rudeness in such a man to kiss such a child. He was tall, and almost stately, with a thoughtful forehead, bright eyes, eagle nose, and gentle mouth; while the princess was such as I have described her.

Not content with being set down and let alone, she continued to storm and scold at the shepherd, crying she was a princess, and would like to know what right he had to touch her! But he only looked down upon her from the height of his tall person with a benignant smile, regarding her as a spoiled little ape whose mother had flattered her by calling her a princess.

"Turn her out of doors, the ungrateful hussy!" cried his wife. "With your bread and your milk inside her ugly body, this is what she gives you for it! Troth, I'm paid for carrying home such an ill-bred tramp in my arms! My own poor angel Agnes! As if that ill-tempered toad were one hair like her!"

These words drove the princess beside herself; for those who are most given to abuse can least endure it. With fists and feet and teeth, as was her wont, she rushed at the shepherdess, whose hand was already raised to deal her a sound box on the ear, when a better appointed minister of vengeance suddenly showed himself. Bounding in at the cottage-door came one of the sheep-dogs, who was called Prince, and whom I shall not refer to with a *which,* because he was a very superior animal indeed, even for a sheep-dog, which is the most intelligent of dogs: he flew at the princess, knocked her down, and commenced shaking her so violently as to tear her miserable clothes to pieces. Used,

however, to mouthing little lambs, he took care not
to hurt her much, though for her good he left her
a blue nip or two by way of letting her imagine
what biting might be. His master, knowing he would
not injure her, thought it better not to call him off,
and in half a minute he left her of his own accord,
and, casting a glance of indignant rebuke behind
him as he went, walked slowly to the hearth, where
he laid himself down with his tail toward her. She
rose, terrified almost to death, and would have crept
again into Agnes's crib for refuge; but the shepherdess cried—

"Come, come, princess! I'll have no skulking to
bed in the good daylight. Go and clean your master's Sunday boots there."

"I will not!" screamed the princess, and ran from
the house.

"Prince!" cried the shepherdess, and up jumped
the dog, and looked in her face, wagging his bushy
tail.

"Fetch her back," she said, pointing to the door.

With two or three bounds Prince caught the
princess, again threw her down, and taking her by
her clothes dragged her back into the cottage, and
dropped her at his mistress' feet, where she lay like
a bundle of rags.

"Get up," said the shepherdess.

Rosamond got up as pale as death.

"Go and clean the boots."

"I don't know how."

"Go and try. There are the brushes, and yonder
is the blacking-pot."

Instructing her how to black boots, it came into
the thought of the shepherdess what a fine thing
it would be if she could teach this miserable little
wretch, so forsaken and ill-bred, to be a good, well-
behaved, respectable child. She was hardly the woman to do it, but every thing well meant is a help,

and she had the wisdom to beg her husband to place Prince under her orders for a while, and not take him to the hill as usual, that he might help her in getting the princess into order.

When the husband was gone, and his boots, with the aid of her own finishing touches, at last quite respectably brushed, the shepherdess told the princess that she might go and play for a while, only she must not go out of sight of the cottage-door.

The princess went right gladly, with the firm intention, however, of getting out of sight by slow degrees, and then at once taking to her heels. But no sooner was she over the threshold than the shepherdess said to the dog, "Watch her;" and out shot Prince.

The moment she saw him, Rosamond threw herself on her face, trembling from head to foot. But the dog had no quarrel with her, and of the violence against which he always felt bound to protest in dog fashion, there was no sign in the prostrate shape before him; so he poked his nose under her, turned her over, and began licking her face and hands. When she saw that he meant to be friendly, her love for animals, which had had no indulgence for a long time now, came wide awake, and in a little while they were romping and rushing about, the best friends in the world.

Having thus seen one enemy, as she thought, changed to a friend, she began to resume her former plan, and crept cunningly farther and farther. At length she came to a little hollow, and instantly rolled down into it. Finding then that she was out of sight of the cottage, she ran off at full speed.

But she had not gone more than a dozen paces, when she heard a growling rush behind her, and the next instant was on the ground, with the dog standing over her, showing his teeth, and flaming at her with his eyes. She threw her arms round his neck, and immediately he licked her face, and let her get up. But the moment she would have moved a step farther from the cottage, there he was in front of her, growling, and showing his teeth. She saw it was of no use, and went back with him.

Thus was the princess provided with a dog for a private tutor—just the right sort for her.

Presently the shepherdess appeared at the door and called her. She would have disregarded the summons, but Prince did his best to let her know that, until she could obey herself, she must obey him. So she went into the cottage, and there the shepherdess ordered her to peel the potatoes for dinner. She sulked and refused. Here Prince could do nothing to help his mistress, but she had not to go far to find another ally.

"Very well, Miss Princess!" she said; "we shall soon see how you like to go without when dinner-time comes."

Now the princess had very little foresight, and the idea of future hunger would have moved her little; but happily, from her game of romps with Prince, she had begun to be hungry already, and so the threat had force. She took the knife and began to peel the potatoes.

By slow degrees the princess improved a little. A few more outbreaks of passion, and a few more savage attacks from Prince, and she had learned to try to restrain herself when she felt the passion coming on; while a few dinnerless afternoons entirely opened her eyes to the necessity of working in order to eat. Prince was her first, and Hunger her second dog-counsellor.

But a still better thing was that she soon grew very fond of Prince. Towards the gaining of her affections, he had three advantages: first, his nature was inferior to hers; next, he was a beast; and last, she was afraid of him; for so spoiled was she that she could more easily love what was below than what was above her, and a beast, than one of her own kind, and indeed could hardly have ever come to love any thing much that she had not first learned to fear, and the white teeth and flaming eyes of the angry Prince were more terrible to her than any thing had yet been, except those of the wolf, which she had now forgotten. Then again, he was such a delightful playfellow, that so long as she neither lost her temper, nor went against orders, she might do almost any thing she pleased with him. In fact, such was his influence upon her, that she who had scoffed at the wisest woman in the whole world, and derided the wishes of her own father and mother, came at length to regard this dog as a superior being, and to look up to him as well as love him. And this was best of all.

The improvement upon her, in the course of a month, was plain. She had quite ceased to go into passions, and had actually begun to take a little interest in her work and try to do it well.

Still, the change was mostly an outside one. I do not mean that she was pretending. Indeed she had never been given to pretence of any sort. But the change was not in *her,* only in her mood. A second change of circumstances would have soon brought a second change of behavior; and, so long as that was possible, she continued the same sort of person she had always been. But if she had not gained much, a trifle had been gained for her: a little quietness and order of mind, and hence a somewhat greater possibility of the first idea of right arising in it, whereupon she would begin to see what a wretched creature she was, and must continue until she herself was right.

Meantime the wise woman had been watching her when she least fancied it, and taking note of the change that was passing upon her. Out of the large

eyes of a gentle sheep she had been watching her—
a sheep that puzzled the shepherd; for every now
and then she would appear in his flock, and he
would catch sight of her two or three times in a
day, sometimes for days together, yet he never saw
her when he looked for her, and never when he
counted the flock into the fold at night. He knew
she was not one of his; but where could she come
from, and where could she go to? For there was no
other flock within many miles, and he never could get
near enough to her to see whether or not she was
marked. Nor was Prince of the least use to him for
the unravelling of the mystery; for although, as often
as he told him to fetch the strange sheep, he went
bounding to her at once, it was only to lie down
at her feet.

At length, however, the wise woman had made
up her mind, and after that the strange sheep no
longer troubled the shepherd.

As Rosamond improved, the shepherdess grew
kinder. She gave her all Agnes's clothes, and began
to treat her much more like a daughter. Hence she
had a great deal of liberty after the little work required of her was over, and would often spend hours
at a time with the shepherd, watching the sheep
and the dogs, and learning a little from seeing how
Prince, and the others as well, managed their charge
—how they never touched the sheep that did as
they were told and turned when they were bid, but
jumped on a disobedient flock, and ran along their
backs, biting, and barking, and half choking themselves with mouthfuls of their wool.

Then also she would play with the brooks, and
learn their songs, and build bridges over them. And
sometimes she would be seized with such delight of
heart that she would spread out her arms to the
wind, and go rushing up the hill till her breath left

her, when she would tumble down in the heather, and lie there till it came back again.

A noticeable change had by this time passed also on her countenance. Her coarse shapeless mouth had begun to show a glimmer of lines and curves about it, and the fat had not returned with the roses to her cheeks, so that her eyes looked larger than before; while, more noteworthy still, the bridge of her nose had grown higher, so that it was less of the impudent, insignificant thing inherited from a certain great-great-great-grandmother, who had little else to leave her. For a long time, it had fitted her very well, for it was just like her; but now there was ground for alteration, and already the granny who gave it her would not have recognized it. It was growing a little like Prince's; and Prince's was a long, perceptive, sagacious nose,—one that was seldom mistaken.

One day about noon, while the sheep were mostly lying down, and the shepherd, having left them to the care of the dogs, was himself stretched under the shade of a rock a little way apart, and the princess sat knitting, with Prince at her feet, lying in wait for a snap at a great fly, for even he had his follies—Rosamond saw a poor woman come toiling up the hill, but took little notice of her until she was passing, a few yards off, when she heard her utter the dog's name in a low voice.

Immediately on the summons, Prince started up and followed her—with hanging head, but gently-wagging tail. At first the princess thought he was merely taking observations, and consulting with his nose whether she was respectable or not, but she soon saw that he was following her in meek submission. Then she sprung to her feet and cried, "Prince, Prince!" But Prince only turned his head and gave her an odd look, as if he were trying to smile, and could not. Then the princess grew angry, and ran

after him, shouting, "Prince, come here directly."
Again Prince turned his head, but this time to growl
and show his teeth.

The princess flew into one of her forgotten rages,
and picking up a stone, flung it at the woman.
Prince turned and darted at her, with fury in his
eyes, and his white teeth gleaming. At the awful
sight the princess turned also, and would have fled,
but he was upon her in a moment, and threw her
to the ground, and there she lay.

It was evening when she came to herself. A cool
twilight wind, that somehow seemed to come all the
way from the stars, was blowing upon her. The poor
woman and Prince, the shepherd and his sheep, were
all gone, and she was left alone with the wind upon
the heather.

She felt sad, weak, and, perhaps, for the first
time in her life, a little ashamed. The violence of
which she had been guilty had vanished from her
spirit, and now lay in her memory with the calm
morning behind it, while in front the quiet dusky
night was now closing in the loud shame betwixt a
double peace. Between the two her passion looked
ugly. It pained her to remember. She felt it was
hateful, and *hers*.

But, alas, Prince was gone! That horrid woman
had taken him away! The fury rose again in her
heart, and raged—until it came to her mind how
her dear Prince would have flown at her throat if
he had seen her in such a passion. The memory
calmed her, and she rose and went home. There,
perhaps, she would find Prince, for surely he could
never have been such a silly dog as go away altogether with a strange woman!

She opened the door and went in. Dogs were
asleep all about the cottage, it seemed to her, but
nowhere was Prince. She crept away to her little
bed, and cried herself asleep.

In the morning the shepherd and shepherdess were indeed glad to find she had come home, for they thought she had run away.

"Where is Prince?" she cried, the moment she waked.

"His mistress has taken him," answered the shepherd.

"Was that woman his mistress?"

"I fancy so. He followed her as if he had known her all his life. I am very sorry to lose him, though."

The poor woman had gone close past the rock where the shepherd lay. He saw her coming, and thought of the strange sheep which had been feeding beside him when he lay down. "Who can she be?" he said to himself; but when he noted how Prince followed her, without even looking up at him as he passed, he remembered how Prince had come to him. And this was how: as he lay in bed one fierce winter morning, just about to rise, he heard the voice of a woman call to him through the storm, "Shepherd, I have brought you a dog. Be good to him. I will come again and fetch him away." He dressed as quickly as he could, and went to the door. It was half snowed up, but on the top of the white mound before it stood Prince. And now he had gone as mysteriously as he had come, and he felt sad.

Rosamond was very sorry too, and hence when she saw the looks of the shepherd and shepherdess, she was able to understand them. And she tried for a while to behave better to them because of their sorrow. So the loss of the dog brought them all nearer to each other.

X

After the thunder-storm, Agnes did not meet with a single obstruction or misadventure. Everybody was strangely polite, gave her whatever she desired, and answered her questions, but asked none in return, and looked all the time as if her departure would be a relief. They were afraid, in fact, from her appearance, lest she should tell them that she was lost, when they would be bound, on pain of public execution, to take her to the palace.

But no sooner had she entered the city than she saw it would hardly do to present herself as a lost child at the palace-gates; for how were they to know that she was not an impostor, especially since she really was one, having run away from the wise woman? So she wandered about looking at every thing until she was tired, and bewildered by the noise and confusion all around her. The wearier she got, the more was she pushed in every direction. Having been used to a whole hill to wander upon, she was very awkward in the crowded streets, and often on the point of being run over by the horses, which seemed to her to be going every way like a frightened flock. She spoke to several persons, but no one stopped to answer her; and at length, her courage giving way, she felt lost indeed, and began to cry. A soldier saw her, and asked what was the matter.

"I've nowhere to go to," she sobbed.

"Where's your mother?" asked the soldier.

"I don't know," answered Agnes. "I was carried

off by an old woman, who then went away and left me. I don't know where she is, or where I am myself."

"Come," said the soldier, "this is a case for his Majesty."

So saying, he took her by the hand, led her to the palace, and begged an audience of the king and queen. The porter glanced at Agnes, immediately admitted them, and showed them into a great splendid room, where the king and queen sat every day to review lost children, in the hope of one day thus finding their Rosamond. But they were by this time beginning to get tired of it. The moment they cast their eyes upon Agnes, the queen threw back her head, threw up her hands, and cried, "What a miserable, conceited, white-faced little ape!" and the king turned upon the soldier in wrath, and cried, forgetting his own decree, "What do you mean by bringing such a dirty, vulgar-looking, pert creature into my palace? The dullest soldier in my army could never for a moment imagine a child like *that*, one hair's-breadth like the lovely angel we lost!"

"I humbly beg your Majesty's pardon," said the soldier, "but what was I to do? There stands your Majesty's proclamation in gold letters on the brazen gates of the palace."

"I shall have it taken down," said the king. "Remove the child."

"Please your Majesty, what am I to do with her?"

"Take her home with you."

"I have six already, sire, and do not want her."

"Then drop her where you picked her up."

"If I do, sire, some one else will find her, and bring her back to your Majesties."

"That will never do," said the king. "I cannot bear to look at her."

"For all her ugliness," said the queen, "she is plainly lost, and so is our Rosamond."

"It may be only a pretence, to get into the palace," said the king.

"Take her to the head scullion, soldier," said the queen, "and tell her to make her useful. If she should find out she has been pretending to be lost, she must let me know."

The soldier was so anxious to get rid of her, that he caught her up in his arms, hurried her from the room, found his way to the scullery, and gave her, trembling with fear, in charge to the head maid, with the queen's message.

As it was evident that the queen had no favor for her, the servants did as they pleased with her, and often treated her harshly. Not one amongst them liked her, nor was it any wonder, seeing that, with every step she took from the wise woman's house, she had grown more contemptible, for she had grown more conceited. Every civil answer given her, she attributed to the impression she made, not to the desire to get rid of her; and every kindness, to approbation of her looks and speech, instead of friendliness to a lonely child. Hence by this time she was twice as odious as before; for whoever has had such severe treatment as the wise woman gave her, and is not the better for it, always grows worse than before. They drove her about, boxed her ears on the smallest provocation, laid every thing to her charge, called her all manner of contemptuous names, jeered and scoffed at her awkwardnesses, and made her life so miserable that she was in a fair way to forget every thing she had learned, and know nothing but how to clean saucepans and kettles.

They would not have been so hard upon her, however, but for her irritating behavior. She dared not refuse to do as she was told, but she obeyed now with a pursed-up mouth, and now with a contemptuous smile. The only thing that sustained her was her constant contriving how to get out of the painful position in which she found herself. There is but one true way, however, of getting out of any position we may be in, and that is, to do the work of it so well that we grow fit for a better: I need not say this was not the plan upon which Agnes was cunning enough to fix.

She had soon learned from the talk around her the reason of the proclamation which had brought her hither.

"Was the lost princess so very beautiful?" she said one day to the youngest of her fellow-servants.

"Beautiful!" screamed the maid; "she was just the ugliest little toad you ever set eyes upon."

"What was she like?" asked Agnes.

"She was about your size, and quite as ugly, only not in the same way; for she had red cheeks, and a cocked little nose, and the biggest, ugliest mouth you ever saw."

Agnes fell a-thinking.

"Is there a picture of her anywhere in the palace?" she asked.

"How should I know? You can ask a housemaid."

Agnes soon learned that there was one, and contrived to get a peep of it. Then she was certain of what she had suspected from the description given of her, namely, that she was the same she had seen in the picture at the wise woman's house. The conclusion followed, that the lost princess must be staying with her father and mother, for assuredly in the picture she wore one of her frocks.

She went to the head scullion, and with humble manner, but proud heart, begged her to procure for her the favor of a word with the queen.

"A likely thing indeed!" was the answer, accompanied by a resounding box on the ear.

She tried the head cook next, but with no better success, and so was driven to her meditations again, the result of which was that she began to drop hints that she knew something about the princess. This came at length to the queen's ears, and she sent for her.

Absorbed in her own selfish ambitions, Agnes never thought of the risk to which she was about to expose her parents, but told the queen that in her wanderings she had caught sight of just such a lovely creature as she described the princess, only dressed like a peasant—saying, that, if the king would permit her to go and look for her, she had little doubt of bringing her back safe and sound within a few weeks.

But although she spoke the truth, she had such a look of cunning on her pinched face, that the queen could not possibly trust her, but believed that she made the proposal merely to get away, and have money given her for her journey. Still there was a chance, and she would not say anything until she had consulted the king.

Then they had Agnes up before the lord chancellor, who, after much questioning of her, arrived at last, he thought, at some notion of the part of the country described by her—that was, if she spoke the truth, which, from her looks and behavior, he also considered entirely doubtful. Thereupon she was ordered back to the kitchen, and a band of soldiers, under a clever lawyer, sent out to search every foot of the supposed region. They were commanded not to return until they brought with them, bound hand and foot, such a shepherd pair as that of which they received a full description.

And now Agnes was worse off than before. For to her other miseries was added the fear of what would befall her when it was discovered that the persons of whom they were in quest, and whom she was certain they must find, were her own father and mother.

By this time the king and queen were so tired of seeing lost children, genuine or pretended—for they cared for no child any longer than there seemed a chance of its turning out their child—that with this new hope, which, however poor and vague at first, soon began to grow upon such imaginations as they had, they commanded the proclamation to be taken down from the palace gates, and directed the various sentries to admit no child whatever, lost or found, be the reason or pretence what it might, until further orders.

"I'm sick of children!" said the king to his secretary, as he finished dictating the direction.

XI

After Prince was gone, the princess, by degrees, fell back into some of her bad old ways, from which only the presence of the dog, not her own betterment, had kept her. She never grew nearly so selfish again, but she began to let her angry old self lift up its head once more, until by and by she grew so bad that the shepherdess declared she should not stop in the house a day longer, for she was quite unendurable.

"It is all very well for you, husband," she said, "for you haven't her all day about you, and only see the best of her. But if you had her in work instead of play hours, you would like her no better than I do. And then it's not her ugly passions only, but when she's in one of her tantrums, it's impossible to get any work out of her. At such times she's just as obstinate as—as—as"—

She was going to say "as Agnes," but the feelings of a mother overcame her, and she could not utter the words.

"In fact," she said instead, "she makes my life miserable."

The shepherd felt he had no right to tell his wife she must submit to have her life made miserable, and therefore, although he was really much attached to Rosamond, he would not interfere; and the shepherdess told her she must look out for another place.

The princess was, however, this much better than before, even in respect of her passions, that they were not quite so bad, and after one was over, she was really ashamed of it. But not once, ever since the departure of Prince, had she tried to check the rush of the evil temper when it came upon her. She hated it when she was out of it, and that was something; but while she was in it, she went full swing with it wherever the prince of the power of it pleased to carry her. Nor was this all: although she might by this time have known well enough that as soon as she was out of it she was certain to be ashamed of it, she would yet justify it to herself with twenty different arguments that looked very good at the time, but would have looked very poor indeed afterwards, if then she had ever remembered them.

She was not sorry to leave the shepherd's cottage, for she felt certain of soon finding her way back to her father and mother; and she would, indeed, have set out long before, but that her foot had somehow got hurt when Prince gave her his last admonition, and she had never since been able for long walks, which she sometimes blamed as the cause of her temper growing worse. But if people are good-tempered only when they are comfortable, what thanks have they?—Her foot was now much better; and as soon as the shepherdess had thus spoken, she resolved to set out at once, and work or beg her way home. At the moment she was quite unmindful of what she owed the good people, and, indeed, was as yet incapable of understanding a tenth part of her obligation to them. So she bade them good by without a tear, and limped her way down the hill, leaving the shepherdess weeping, and the shepherd looking very grave.

When she reached the valley she followed the course of the stream, knowing only that it would lead her away from the hill where the sheep fed, into richer lands where there were farms and cattle. Rounding one of the roots of the hill she saw before her a poor woman walking slowly along the road with a burden of heather upon her back, and presently passed her, but had gone only a few paces farther when she heard her calling after her in a kind old voice—

"Your shoe-tie is loose, my child."

But Rosamond was growing tired, for her foot had become painful, and so she was cross, and neither returned answer, nor paid heed to the warning. For when we are cross, all our other faults grow busy, and poke up their ugly heads like maggots, and the princess's old dislike to doing any thing that came to her with the least air of advice about it returned in full force.

"My child," said the woman again, "if you don't fasten your shoe-tie, it will make you fall."

"Mind your own business," said Rosamond, without even turning her head, and had not gone more than three steps when she fell flat on her face on the path. She tried to get up, but the effort forced from her a scream, for she had sprained the ankle of the foot that was already lame.

The old woman was by her side instantly.

"Where are you hurt, child?" she asked, throwing down her burden and kneeling beside her.

"Go away," screamed Rosamond. *"You* made me fall, you bad woman!"

The woman made no reply, but began to feel her joints, and soon discovered the sprain. Then, in spite of Rosamond's abuse, and the violent pushes and even kicks she gave her, she took the hurt ankle in her hands, and stroked and pressed it, gently kneading it, as it were, with her thumbs, as if coaxing every particle of the muscles into its right place. Nor had she done so long before Rosamond lay still. At length she ceased, and said:—

"Now, my child, you may get up."

"I can't get up, and I'm not your child," cried Rosamond. "Go away."

Without another word the woman left her, took up her burden, and continued her journey.

In a little while Rosamond tried to get up, and not only succeeded, but found she could walk, and, indeed, presently discovered that her ankle and foot also were now perfectly well.

"I wasn't much hurt after all," she said to herself, nor sent a single grateful thought after the poor woman, whom she speedily passed once more upon the road without even a greeting.

Late in the afternoon she came to a spot where the path divided into two, and was taking the one she liked the look of better, when she started at the sound of the poor woman's voice, whom she thought she had left far behind, again calling her. She looked round, and there she was, toiling under her load of heather as before.

"You are taking the wrong turn, child," she cried.

"How can you tell that?" said Rosamond. "You know nothing about where I want to go."

"I know that road will take you where you don't want to go," said the woman.

"I shall know when I get there, then," returned Rosamond, "and no thanks to you."

She set off running. The woman took the other path, and was soon out of sight.

By and by, Rosamond found herself in the midst of a peat-moss—a flat, lonely, dismal, black country. She thought, however, that the road would soon lead her across to the other side of it among the farms, and went on without anxiety. But the stream, which had hitherto been her guide, had now vanished; and when it began to grow dark, Rosamond found that she could no longer distinguish the track. She turned, therefore, but only to find that the same darkness covered it behind as well as before. Still she made the attempt to go back by keeping as direct a line as she could, for the path was straight as an arrow. But she could not see enough even to start her in a line, and she had not gone far before she found herself hemmed in, apparently on every side, by ditches and pools of black, dismal, slimy water. And now it was so dark that she could see nothing more than the gleam of a bit of clear sky now and then in the water. Again and again she stepped knee-deep in black mud, and once tumbled down in the shallow edge of a terrible pool; after which she gave up the attempt to escape the meshes of the watery net, stood still, and began to cry bitterly, despairingly. She saw now that her unreasonable anger had made her foolish as well as rude, and felt that she was justly punished for her wickedness to the poor woman who had been so friendly to her. What would Prince think of her, if he knew? She cast herself on the ground, hungry, and cold, and weary.

Presently, she thought she saw long creatures come heaving out of the black pools. A toad jumped upon her, and she shrieked, and sprang to her feet, and would have run away headlong, when she spied in the distance a faint glimmer. She thought it was a Will-o'-the-wisp. What could he be after? Was he looking for her? She dared not run, lest he should see and pounce upon her. The light came nearer, and grew brighter and larger. Plainly, the little fiend was looking for her—he would torment her. After many twistings and turnings among the pools, it came straight towards her, and she would have shrieked, but that terror made her dumb.

It came nearer and nearer, and lo! it was borne by a dark figure, with a burden on its back: it was the poor woman, and no demon, that was looking for her! She gave a scream of joy, fell down weeping at her feet, and clasped her knees. Then the poor woman threw away her burden, laid down her lantern, took the princess up in her arms, folded her cloak around her, and having taken up her lantern again, carried her slowly and carefully through the midst of the black pools, winding hither and thither. All night long she carried her thus, slowly and wearily, until at length the darkness grew a little thinner, an uncertain hint of light came from the east, and the poor woman, stopping on the brow of a little hill, opened her cloak, and set the princess down.

"I can carry you no farther," she said. "Sit there on the grass till the light comes. I will stand here by you."

Rosamond had been asleep. Now she rubbed her eyes and looked, but it was too dark to see any thing more than that there was a sky over her head. Slowly the light grew, until she could see the form of the poor woman standing in front of her; and as it went on growing, she began to think she had seen her somewhere before, till all at once she thought of the wise woman, and saw it must be she. Then she was so ashamed that she bent down her head, and could look at her no longer. But the poor woman spoke, and the voice was that of the wise woman, and every word went deep into the heart of the princess.

"Rosamond," she said, "all this time, ever since I carried you from your father's palace, I have been doing what I could to make you a lovely creature: ask yourself how far I have succeeded."

All her past story, since she found herself first under the wise woman's cloak, arose, and glided past the inner eyes of the princess, and she saw, and in a measure understood, it all. But she sat with her eyes on the ground, and made no sign.

Then said the wise woman:—

"Below there is the forest which surrounds my house. I am going home. If you please to come there to me, I will help you, in a way I could not do now, to be good and lovely. I will wait you there all day, but if you start at once, you may be there long before noon. I shall have your breakfast waiting for you. One thing more: the beasts have not yet all gone home to their holes; but I give you my word, not one will touch you so long as you keep coming nearer to my house."

She ceased. Rosamond sat waiting to hear something more; but nothing came. She looked up; she was alone.

Alone once more! Always being left alone, because she would not yield to what was right! Oh, how safe she had felt under the wise woman's cloak! She had indeed been good to her, and she had in return behaved like one of the hyenas of the awful wood! What a wonderful house it was she lived in! And again all her own story came up into her brain from her repentant heart.

"Why didn't she take me with her?" she said. "I would have gone gladly." And she wept. But her own conscience told her that, in the very middle of her shame and desire to be good, she had returned no answer to the words of the wise woman; she had sat like a tree-stump, and done nothing. She tried to say there was nothing to be done; but she knew at once that she could have told the wise woman she had been very wicked, and asked her to take her with her. Now there was nothing to be done.

"Nothing to be done!" said her conscience. "Cannot you rise, and walk down the hill, and through the wood?"

"But the wild beasts!"

"There it is! You don't believe the wise woman yet! Did she not tell you the beasts would not touch you?"

"But they are so horrid!"

"Yes, they are; but it would be far better to be

eaten up alive by them than live on—such a worthless creature as you are. Why, you're not fit to be thought about by any but bad ugly creatures."

This was how herself talked to her.

XII

All at once she jumped to her feet, and ran at full speed down the hill and into the wood. She heard howlings and yellings on all sides of her, but she ran straight on, as near as she could judge. Her spirits rose as she ran. Suddenly she saw before her, in the dusk of the thick wood, a group of some dozen wolves and hyenas, standing all together right in her way, with their green eyes fixed upon her staring. She faltered one step, then bethought her of what the wise woman had promised, and keeping straight on, dashed right into the middle of them. They fled howling, as if she had struck them with fire. She was no more afraid after that, and ere the sun was up she was out of the wood and upon the heath, which no bad thing could step upon and live. With the first peep of the sun above the horizon, she saw the little cottage before her, and ran as fast as she could run towards it. When she came near it, she saw that the door was open, and ran straight into the outstretched arms of the wise woman.

The wise woman kissed her and stroked her hair, set her down by the fire, and gave her a bowl of bread and milk.

When she had eaten it she drew her before her where she sat, and spoke to her thus:—

"Rosamond, if you would be a blessed creature instead of a mere wretch, you must submit to be tried."

88

"Is that something terrible?" asked the princess, turning white.

"No, my child; but it is something very difficult to come well out of. Nobody who has not been tried knows how difficult it is; but whoever has come well out of it, and those who do not overcome never do come out of it, always looks back with horror, not on what she has come through, but on the very idea of the possibility of having failed, and being still the same miserable creature as before."

"You will tell me what it is before it begins?" said the princess.

"I will not tell you exactly. But I will tell you some things to help you. One great danger is that perhaps you will think you are in it before it has really begun, and say to yourself, 'Oh! this is really nothing to me. It may be a trial to some, but for me I am sure it is not worth mentioning.' And then, before you know, it will be upon you, and you will fail utterly and shamefully."

"I will be very, very careful," said the princess. "Only don't let me be frightened."

"You shall not be frightened, except it be your own doing. You are already a brave girl, and there is no occasion to try you more that way. I saw how you rushed into the middle of the ugly creatures; and as they ran from you, so will all kinds of evil things, as long as you keep them outside of you, and do not open the cottage of your heart to let them in. I will tell you something more about what you will have to go through.

"Nobody can be a real princess—do not imagine you have yet been any thing more than a mock one—until she is a princess over herself, that is, until, when she finds herself unwilling to do the thing that is right, she makes herself do it. So long as any mood she is in makes her do the thing she will be sorry for when that mood is over, she is a

slave, and no princess. A princess is able to do
what is right even should she unhappily be in a
mood that would make another unable to do it. For
instance, if you should be cross and angry, you are
not a whit the less bound to be just, yes, kind even—
a thing most difficult in such a mood—though ease
itself in a good mood, loving and sweet. Whoever
does what she is bound to do, be she the dirtiest
little girl in the street, is a princess, worshipful, hon-
orable. Nay, more; her might goes farther than she
could send it, for if she act so, the evil mood will
will wither and die, and leave her loving and clean.
—Do you understand me, dear Rosamond?"

As she spoke, the wise woman laid her hand on
her head and looked—oh, so lovingly!—into her
eyes.

"I am not sure," said the princess, humbly.

"Perhaps you will understand me better if I say it
just comes to this, that you must *not do* what is
wrong, however much you are inclined to do it, and
you must *do* what is right, however much you are
disinclined to do it."

"I understand that," said the princess.

"I am going, then, to put you in one of the
mood-chambers of which I have many in the house.
Its mood will come upon you, and you will have to
deal with it."

She rose and took her by the hand. The princess
trembled a little, but never thought of resisting.

The wise woman led her into the great hall with
the pictures, and through a door at the farther end,
opening upon another large hall, which was circular, and had doors close to each other all round it.
Of these she opened one, pushed the princess gently
in, and closed it behind her.

The princess found herself in her old nursery.
Her little white rabbit came to meet her in a lump-
ing canter as if his back were going to tumble over

his head. Her nurse, in her rocking-chair by the chimney corner, sat just as she had used. The fire burned brightly, and on the table were many of her wonderful toys, on which, however, she now looked with some contempt. Her nurse did not seem at all surprised to see her, any more than if the princess had but just gone from the room and returned again.

"Oh! how different I am from what I used to be!" thought the princess to herself, looking from her toys to her nurse. "The wise woman has done me so much good already! I will go and see mamma at once, and tell her I am very glad to be at home again, and very sorry I was so naughty."

She went towards the door.

"Your queen-mamma, princess, cannot see you now," said her nurse.

"I have yet to learn that it is my part to take orders from a servant," said the princess with temper and dignity.

"I beg your pardon, princess, returned her nurse, politely; "but it is my duty to tell you that your queen-mamma is at this moment engaged. She is alone with her most intimate friend, the Princess of the Frozen Regions."

"I shall see for myself," returned the princess, bridling, and walked to the door.

Now little bunny, leap-frogging near the door, happened that moment to get about her feet, just as she was going to open it, so that she tripped and fell against it, striking her forehead a good blow. She caught up the rabbit in a rage, and, crying, "It is all your fault, you ugly old wretch!" threw it with violence in her nurse's face.

Her nurse caught the rabbit, and held it to her face, as if seeking to sooth its fright. But the rabbit looked very limp and odd, and, to her amazement, Rosamond presently saw that the thing was no rabbit, but a pocket-handkerchief. The next moment she removed it from her face, and Rosamond beheld —not her nurse, but the wise woman—standing on her own hearth, while she herself stood by the door leading from the cottage into the hall.

"First trial a failure," said the wise woman quietly.

Overcome with shame, Rosamond ran to her, fell down on her knees, and hid her face in her dress.

"Need I say any thing?" said the wise woman, stroking her hair.

"No, no," cried the princess. "I am horrid."

"You know now the kind of thing you have to meet: are you ready to try again?"

"*May* I try again?" cried the princess, jumping up. "I'm ready. I do not think I shall fail this time."

"The trial will be harder."

Rosamond drew in her breath, and set her teeth. The wise woman looked at her pitifully, but took her by the hand, led her to the round hall, opened the same door, and closed it after her.

The princess expected to find herself again in the nursery, but in the wise woman's house no one ever has the same trial twice. She was in a beautiful garden, full of blossoming trees and the loveliest roses and lilies. A lake was in the middle of it, with a tiny boat. So delightful was it that Rosamond forgot all about how or why she had come there, and lost herself in the joy of the flowers and the trees and the water. Presently came the shout of a child, merry and glad, and from a clump of tulip trees rushed a lovely little boy, with his arms stretched out to her. She was charmed at the sight, ran to meet him, caught him up in her arms, kissed him, and could hardly let him go again. But the moment she set him down he ran from her towards the lake, looking back as he ran, and crying "Come, come."

She followed. He made straight for the boat,

clambered into it, and held out his hand to help
her in. Then he caught up the little boat-hook, and
pushed away from the shore: there was a great white
flower floating a few yards off, and that was the
little fellow's goal. But, alas! no sooner had Rosamond caught sight of it, huge and glowing as a
harvest moon, than she felt a great desire to have
it herself. The boy, however, was in the bows of
the boat, and caught it first. It had a long stem,
reaching down to the bottom of the water, and for
a moment he tugged at it in vain, but at last it
gave way so suddenly, that he tumbled back with
the flower into the bottom of the boat. Then Rosamond, almost wild at the danger it was in as he
struggled to rise, hurried to save it, but somehow
between them it came in pieces, and all its petals
of fretted silver were scattered about the boat. When
the boy got up, and saw the ruin his companion
had occasioned, he burst into tears, and having the
long stalk of the flower still in his hand, struck her
with it across the face. It did not hurt her much,
for he was a very little fellow, but it was wet and
slimy. She tumbled rather than rushed at him, seized
him in her arms, tore him from his frightened grasp,
and flung him into the water. His head struck on
the boat as he fell, and he sank at once to the bottom, where he lay looking up at her with white face
and open eyes.

The moment she saw the consequences of her
deed she was filled with horrible dismay. She tried
hard to reach down to him through the water, but
it was far deeper than it looked, and she could not.
Neither could she get her eyes to leave the white
face: its eyes fascinated and fixed hers; and there she
lay leaning over the boat and staring at the death
she had made. But I voice crying, "Ally! Ally!"
shot to her heart, and springing to her feet she saw
a lovely lady come running down the grass to the

brink of the water with her hair flying about her head.

"Where is my Ally?" she shrieked.

But Rosamond could not answer, and only stared at the lady, as she had before stared at her drowned boy.

Then the lady caught sight of the dead thing at the bottom of the water, and rushed in, and, plunging down, struggled and groped until she reached it. Then she rose and stood up with the dead body of her little son in her arms, his head hanging back, and the water streaming from him.

"See what you have made of him, Rosamond!" she said, holding the body out to her; "and this is your second trial, and also a failure."

The dead child melted away from her arms, and there she stood, the wise woman, on her own hearth, while Rosamond found herself beside the little well on the floor of the cottage, with one arm wet up to the shoulder. She threw herself on the heather-bed and wept from relief and vexation both.

The wise woman walked out of the cottage, shut the door, and left her alone. Rosamond was sobbing, so that she did not hear her go. When at length she looked up, and saw that the wise woman was gone, her misery returned afresh and tenfold, and she wept and wailed. The hours passed, the shadows of evening began to fall, and the wise woman entered.

XIII

She went straight to the bed, and taking Rosamond in her arms, sat down with her by the fire.

"My poor child!" she said. "Two terrible failures! And the more the harder! They get stronger and stronger. What is to be done?"

"Couldn't you help me?" said Rosamond piteously.

"Perhaps I could, now you ask me," answered the wise woman. "When you are ready to try again, we shall see."

"I am very tired of myself," said the princess. "But I can't rest till I try again."

"That is the only way to get rid of your weary, shadowy self, and find your strong, true self. Come, my child; I will help you all I can, for now I *can* help you."

Yet again she led her to the same door, and seemed to the princess to send her yet again alone into the room. She was in a forest, a place half wild, half tended. The trees were grand, and full of the loveliest birds, of all glowing gleaming and radiant colors, which, unlike the brilliant birds we know in our world, sang deliciously, every one according to his color. The trees were not at all crowded, but their leaves were so thick, and their boughs spread so far, that it was only here and there a sunbeam could get straight through. All the gentle creatures of a forest were there, but no creatures that killed, not even a weasel to kill the rabbits, or a beetle to eat the snails out of their striped shells.

95

As to the butterflies, words would but wrong them if they tried to tell how gorgeous they were. The princess's delight was so great that she neither laughed nor ran, but walked about with a solemn countenance and stately step.

"But where are the flowers?" she said to herself at length.

They were nowhere. Neither on the high trees, nor on the few shrubs that grew here and there amongst them, were there any blossoms; and in the grass that grew everywhere there was not a single flower to be seen.

"Ah, well!" said Rosamond again to herself, "where all the birds and butterflies are living flowers, we can do without the other sort."

Still she could not help feeling that flowers were wanted to make the beauty of the forest complete.

Suddenly she came out on a little open glade; and there, on the root of a great oak, sat the loveliest little girl, with her lap full of flowers of all colors, but of such kinds as Rosamond had never before seen. She was playing with them—burying her hands in them, tumbling them about, and every now and then picking one from the rest, and throwing it away. All the time she never smiled, except with her eyes, which were as full as they could hold of the laughter of the spirit—a laughter which in this world is never heard, only sets the eyes alight with a liquid shining. Rosamond drew nearer, for the wonderful creature would have drawn a tiger to her side, and tamed him on the way. A few yards from her, she came upon one of her cast-away flowers and stooped to pick it up, as well she might where none grew save in her own longing. But to her amazement she found, instead of a flower thrown away to wither, one fast rooted and quite at home. She left it, and went to another; but it also was fast in the soil, and growing comfortably in the warm grass.

What could it mean? One after another she tried, until at length she was satisfied that it was the same with every flower the little girl threw from her lap.

She watched then until she saw her throw one, and instantly bounded to the spot. But the flower had been quicker than she: there it grew, fast fixed in the earth, and, she thought, looked at her roguishly. Something evil moved in her, and she plucked it.

"Don't! don't!" cried the child. "My flowers cannot live in your hands."

Rosamond looked at the flower. It was withered already. She threw it from her, offended. The child rose, with difficulty keeping her lapful together, picked it up, carried it back, sat down again, spoke to it, kissed it, sang to it—oh! such a sweet, childish little song!—the princess never could recall a word of it—and threw it away. Up rose its little head, and there it was, busy growing again!

Rosamond's bad temper soon gave way: the beauty and sweetness of the child had overcome it; and, anxious to make friends with her, she drew near, and said:

"Won't you give me a little flower, please, you beautiful child?"

"There they are; they are all for you," answered the child, pointing with her outstretched arm and forefinger all round.

"But you told me, a minute ago, not to touch them."

"Yes, indeed, I did."

"They can't be mine, if I'm not to touch them."

"If, to call them yours, you must kill them, then they are not yours, and never, never can be yours. They are nobody's when they are dead."

"But you don't kill them."

"I don't pull them; I throw them away. I live them."

"How is it that you make them grow?"

"I say, 'You darling!' and throw it away and there it is."

"Where do you get them?"

"In my lap."

"I wish you would let me throw one away."

"Have you got any in your lap? Let me see."

"No; I have none."

"Then you can't throw one away, if you haven't got one."

"You are mocking me!" cried the princess.

"I am not mocking you," said the child, looking her full in the face, with reproach in her large blue eyes.

"Oh, that's where the flowers come from!" said the princess to herself, the moment she saw them, hardly knowing what she meant.

Then the child rose as if hurt, and quickly threw away all the flowers she had in her lap, but one by one, and without any sign of anger. When they were all gone, she stood a moment, and then, in a kind of chanting cry, called, two or three times, "Peggy! Peggy! Peggy!"

A low, glad cry, like the whinny of a horse, answered, and, presently, out of the wood on the opposite side of the glade, came gently trotting the loveliest little snow-white pony, with great shining blue wings, half-lifted from his shoulders. Straight towards the little girl, neither hurrying nor lingering, he trotted with light elastic tread.

Rosamond's love for animals broke into a perfect passion of delight at the vision. She rushed to meet the pony with such haste, that, although clearly the best trained animal under the sun, he started back, plunged, reared, and struck out with his fore-feet ere he had time to observe what sort of a creature it was that had so startled him. When he perceived it was a little girl, he dropped instantly upon all fours, and content with avoiding her, resumed his quiet trot in the direction of his mistress. Rosamond stood gazing after him in miserable disappointment.

When he reached the child, he laid his head on her shoulder, and she put her arm up round his neck; and after she had talked to him a little, he turned and came trotting back to the princess.

Almost beside herself with joy, she began caressing him in the rough way which, notwithstanding her love for them, she was in the habit of using with animals; and she was not gentle enough, in herself even, to see that he did not like it, and was only putting up with it for the sake of his mistress. But when, that she might jump upon his back, she laid hold of one of his wings, and ruffled some of the blue feathers, he wheeled suddenly about, gave his long tail a sharp whisk which threw her flat on the grass, and, trotting back to his mistress, bent down his head before her as if asking excuse for ridding himself of the unbearable.

The princess was furious. She had forgotten all her past life up to the time when she first saw the child: her beauty had made her forget, and yet she was now on the very borders of hating her. What she might have done, or rather tried to do, had not Peggy's tail struck her down with such force that for a moment she could not rise, I cannot tell.

But while she lay half-stunned, her eyes fell on a little flower just under them. It stared up in her face like the living thing it was, and she could not take her eyes off its face. It was like a primrose trying to express doubt instead of confidence. It seemed to put her half in mind of something, and she felt as if shame were coming. She put out her hand to pluck it; but the moment her fingers touched it, the flower withered up, and hung as dead on its stalks as if a flame of fire had passed over it.

Then a shudder thrilled through the heart of the

princess, and she thought with herself, saying—
"What sort of a creature am I that the flowers wither
when I touch them, and the ponies despise me with
their tails? What a wretched, coarse, ill-bred creature I must be! There is that lovely child giving life
instead of death to the flowers, and a moment ago I
was hating her! I am made horrid, and I shall be
horrid, and I hate myself, and yet I can't help
being myself!"

She heard the sound of galloping feet, and there
was the pony, with the child seated betwixt his
wings, coming straight on at full speed for where
she lay.

"I don't care," she said. "They may trample me
under their feet if they like. I am tired and sick of
myself—a creature at whose touch the flowers
wither!"

On came the winged pony. But while yet some
distance off, he gave a great bound, spread out his
living sails of blue, rose yards and yards above her
in the air, and alighted as gently as a bird, just a
few feet on the other side of her. The child slipped
down and came and kneeled over her.

"Did my pony hurt you?" she said. "I am so
sorry!"

"Yes, he hurt me," answered the princess, "but
not more than I deserved, for I took liberties with
him, and he did not like it."

"Oh, you dear!" said the little girl. "I love you for
talking so of my Peggy. He is a good pony, though a
little playful sometimes. Would you like a ride upon
him?"

"You darling beauty!" cried Rosamond, sobbing.
"I do love you so, you are so good. How did you
became so sweet?"

"Would you like to ride my pony?" repeated the
child, with a heavenly smile in her eyes.

"No, no; he is fit only for you. My clumsy body would hurt him," said Rosamond.

"You don't mind me having such a pony?" said the child.

"What! mind it?" cried Rosamond, almost indignantly. Then remembering certain thoughts that had but a few moments before passed through her mind, she looked on the ground and was silent.

"You don't mind it, then?" repeated the child.

"I am very glad there is such a you and such a pony, and that such a you has got such a pony," said Rosamond, still looking on the ground. "But I do wish the flowers would not die when I touch them. I was cross to see you make them grow, but now I should be content if only I did not make them wither."

As she spoke, she stroked the little girl's bare feet, which were by her, half buried in the soft moss, and as she ended she laid her cheek on them and kissed them.

"Dear princess!" said the little girl, "the flowers will not always wither at your touch. Try now—only do not pluck it. Flowers ought never to be plucked except to give away. Touch it gently."

A silvery flower, something like a snowdrop, grew just within her reach. Timidly she stretched out her hand and touched it. The flower trembled, but neither shrank nor withered.

"Touch it again," said the child.

It changed color a little, and Rosamond fancied it grew larger.

"Touch it again," said the child.

It opened and grew until it was as large as a narcissus, and changed and deepened in color till it was a red glowing gold.

Rosamond gazed motionless. When the transfiguration of the flower was perfected, she sprang to her feet with clasped hands, but for very ecstasy of joy stood speechless, gazing at the child.

"Did you never see me before, Rosamond?" she asked.

"No, never," answered the princess. "I never saw any thing half so lovely."

"Look at me," said the child.

And as Rosamond looked, the child began, like the flower, to grow larger. Quickly through every gradation of growth she passed, until she stood before her a woman perfectly beautiful, neither old nor young; for hers was the old age of everlasting youth.

Rosamond was utterly enchanted, and stood gazing without word or movement until she could endure no more delight. Then her mind collapsed to the thought—had the pony grown too? She glanced round. There was no pony, no grass, no flowers, no bright-birded forest—but the cottage of the wise woman—and before her, on the hearth of it, the goddess-child, the only thing unchanged.

She gasped with astonishment.

"You must set out for your father's palace immediately," said the lady.

"But where is the wise woman?" asked Rosamond, looking all about.

"Here," said the lady.

And Rosamond, looking again, saw the wise woman, folded as usual in her long dark cloak.

"And it was you all the time?" she cried in delight, and kneeled before her, burying her face in her garments.

"It always is me, all the time," said the wise woman, smiling.

"But which is the real you?" asked Rosamond; "this or that?"

"Or a thousand others?" returned the wise woman. "But the one you have just seen is the likest to the real me that you are able to see just yet—but—. And that me you could not have seen a little while ago.—But, my darling child," she went on, lifting her up and clasping her to her bosom, "you must not think, because you have seen me once, that therefore you are capable of seeing me at all times. No; there are many things in you yet that must be changed before that can be. Now, however, you will seek me. Every time you feel you want me, that is a sign I am wanting you. There are yet many rooms in my house you may have to go through; but when you need no more of them, then you will be able to throw flowers like the little girl you saw in the forest."

The princess gave a sigh.

"Do not think," the wise woman went on, "that the things you have seen in my house are mere empty shadows. You do not know, you cannot yet think, how living and true they are.—Now you must go."

She led her once more into the great hall, and there showed her the picture of her father's capital, and his palace with the brazen gates.

"There is your home," she said. "Go to it."

The princess understood, and a flush of shame rose to her forehead. She turned to the wise woman and said:

"Will you forgive *all* my naughtiness, and *all* the trouble I have given you?"

"If I had not forgiven you, I would never have taken the trouble to punish you. If I had not loved you, do you think I would have carried you away in my cloak?"

"How could you love such an ugly, ill-tempered, rude, hateful little wretch?"

"I saw, through it all, what you were going to be," said the wise woman, kissing her. "But remember you have yet only *begun* to be what I saw."

"I will try to remember," said the princess, holding her cloak, and looking up in her face.

"Go, then," said the wise woman.

Rosamond turned away on the instant, ran to the picture, stepped over the frame of it, heard a door close gently, gave one glance back, saw behind her the loveliest palace-front of alabaster, gleaming in the pale-yellow light of an early summer-morning, looked again to the eastward, saw the faint outline of her father's city against the sky, and ran off to reach it.

It looked much further off now than when it seemed a picture, but the sun was not yet up, and she had the whole of a summer day before her.

XIV

The soldiers sent out by the king, had no great difficulty in finding Agnes's father and mother, of whom they demanded if they knew any thing of such a young princess as they described. The honest pair told them the truth in every point—that, having lost their own child and found another, they had taken her home, and treated her as their own; that she had indeed called herself a princess, but they had not believed her, because she did not look like one; that, even if they had, they did not know how they could have done differently, seeing they were poor people, who could not afford to keep any idle person about the place; that they had done their best to teach her good ways, and had not parted with her until her bad temper rendered it impossible to put up with her any longer; that, as to the king's proclamation, they heard little of the world's news on their lonely hill, and it had never reached them; that if it had, they did not know how either of them could have gone such a distance from home, and left their sheep or their cottage, one or the other, uncared for.

"You must learn, then, how both of you can go, and your sheep must take care of your cottage," said the lawyer, and commanded the soldiers to bind them hand and foot.

Heedless of their entreaties to be spared such an indignity, the soldiers obeyed, bore them to a cart, and set out for the king's palace, leaving the cottage door open, the fire burning, the pot of potatoes boiling upon it, the sheep scattered over the hill, and the dogs not knowing what to do.

Hardly were they gone, however, before the wise woman walked up, with Prince behind her, peeped into the cottage, locked the door, put the key in her pocket, and then walked away up the hill. In a few minutes there arose a great battle between Prince and the dog which filled his former place—a well-meaning but dull fellow, who could fight better than feed. Prince was not long in showing him that he was meant for his master, and then, by his efforts, and directions to the other dogs, the sheep were soon gathered again, and out of danger from foxes and bad dogs. As soon as this was done, the wise woman left them in charge of Prince, while she went to the next farm to arrange for the folding of the sheep, and the feeding of the dogs.

When the soldiers reached the palace, they were ordered to carry their prisoners at once into the presence of the king and queen, in the throne room. Their two thrones stood upon a high dais at one end, and on the floor at the foot of the dais, the soldiers laid their helpless prisoners. The queen commanded that they should be unbound, and ordered them to stand up. They obeyed with the dignity of insulted innocence, and their bearing offended their foolish majesties.

Meantime the princess, after a long day's journey, arrived at the palace, and walked up to the sentry at the gate.

"Stand back," said the sentry.

"I wish to go in, if you please," said the princess gently.

"Ha! ha! ha!" laughed the sentry, for he was one of those dull people who form their judgment from a person's clothes, without even looking in his eyes; and as the princess happened to be in rags, her request was amusing, and the booby thought himself quite clever for laughing at her so thoroughly.

"I am the princess," Rosamond said quietly.

"What princess?" bellowed the man.

"The princess Rosamond. Is there another?" she answered and asked.

But the man was so tickled at the wondrous idea of a princess in rags, that he scarcely heard what she said for laughing. As soon as he recovered a little, he proceeded to chuck the princess under the chin, saying—

"You're a pretty girl, my dear, though you ain't no princess."

Rosamond drew back with dignity.

"You have spoken three untruths at once," she said. "I am *not* pretty, and I *am* a princess, and if I were dear to you, as I ought to be, you would not laugh at me because I am badly dressed, but stand aside, and let me go to my father and mother."

The tone of her speech, and the rebuke she gave him, made the man look at her; and looking at her, he began to tremble inside his foolish body, and wonder whether he might not have made a mistake. He raised his hand in salute, and said—

"I beg your pardon, miss, but I have express orders to admit no child whatever within the palace gates. They tell me his majesty the king says he is sick of children."

"He may well be sick of me!" thought the princess; "but it can't mean that he does not want me home again.—I don't think you can very well call me a child," she said, looking the sentry full in the face.

"You ain't very big, miss," answered the soldier, "but so be you say you ain't a child, I'll take the risk. The king can only kill me, and a man must die once."

He opened the gate, stepped aside, and allowed

her to pass. Had she lost her temper, as every one but the wise woman would have expected of her, he certainly would not have done so.

She ran into the palace, the door of which had been left open by the porter when he followed the soldiers and prisoners to the throne-room, and bounded up the stairs to look for her father and mother. As she passed the door of the throne-room she heard an unusual noise in it, and running to the king's private entrance, over which hung a heavy curtain, she peeped past the edge of it, and saw, to her amazement, the shepherd and shepherdess standing like culprits before the king and queen, and the same moment heard the king say—

"Peasants, where is the princess Rosamond?"

"Truly, sire, we do not know," answered the shepherd.

"You ought to know," said the king.

"Sire, we could keep her no longer."

"You confess, then," said the king, suppressing the outbreak of the wrath that boiled up in him, "that you turned her out of your house."

For the king had been informed by a swift messenger of all that had passed long before the arrival of the prisoners.

"We did, sire; but not only could we keep her no longer, but we knew not that she was the princess."

"You ought to have known, the moment you cast your eyes upon her," said the king. "Any one who does not know a princess the moment he sees her, ought to have his eyes put out."

"Indeed he ought," said the queen.

To this they returned no answer, for they had none ready.

"Why did you not bring her at once to the palace," pursued the king, "whether you knew her to be a princess or not? My proclamation left nothing to your judgment. It said *every child*."

"We heard nothing of the proclamation, sire."

"You ought to have heard," said the king. "It is enough that I make proclamations; it is for you to read them. Are they not written in letters of gold upon the brazen gates of this palace?"

"A poor shepherd, your majesty—how often must he leave his flock, and go hundreds of miles to look whether there may not be something in letters of gold upon the brazen gates? We did not know that your majesty had made a proclamation, or even that the princess was lost."

"You ought to have known," said the king.

The shepherd held his peace.

"But," said the queen, taking up the word, "all that is as nothing, when I think how you misused the darling."

The only ground the queen had for saying thus, was what Agnes had told her as to how the princess was dressed; and her condition seemed to the queen so miserable, that she had imagined all sorts of oppression and cruelty.

But this was more than the shepherdess, who had not yet spoken, could bear.

"She would have been dead, and *not* buried, long ago, madam, if I had not carried her home in my two arms."

"Why does she say her *two* arms?" said the king to himself. "Has she more than two? Is there treason in that?"

"You dressed her in cast-off clothes," said the queen.

"I dressed her in my own sweet child's Sunday clothes. And this is what I get for it!" cried the shepherdess, bursting into tears.

"And what did you do with the clothes you took off her? Sell them?"

"Put them in the fire, madam. They were not fit for the poorest child in the mountains. They were so ragged that you could see her skin through them in twenty different places."

"You cruel woman, to torture a mother's feelings so!" cried the queen, and in her turn burst into tears.

"And I'm sure," sobbed the shepherdess, "I took every pains to teach her what it was right for her to know. I taught her to tidy the house, and"—

"Tidy the house?" moaned the queen. "My poor wretched offspring!"

"And peel the potatoes, and"—

"Peel the potatoes!" cried the queen. "Oh, horror!"

"And black her master's boots," said the shepherdess.

"Black her master's boots!" shrieked the queen. "Oh, my white-handed princess! Oh, my ruined baby!"

"What I want to know," said the king, paying no heed to this maternal duel, but patting the top of his sceptre as if it had been the hilt of a sword which he was about to draw, "is, where the princess is now."

The shepherd made no answer, for he had nothing to say more than he had said already.

"You have murdered her!" shouted the king. "You shall be tortured till you confess the truth; and then you shall be tortured to death, for you are the most abominable wretches in the whole wide world."

"Who accuses me of crime?" cried the shepherd, indignant.

"I accuse you," said the king; "but you shall see, face to face, the chief witness to your villany. Officer, bring the girl."

Silence filled the hall while they waited. The king's face was swollen with anger. The queen hid hers behind her handkerchief. The shepherd and shepherdess bent their eyes on the ground, wondering. It was with difficulty Rosamond could keep her place, but so wise had she already become that she saw it would be far better to let every thing come out before she interfered.

At length the door opened, and in came the officer, followed by Agnes, looking white as death and mean as sin.

The shepherdess gave a shriek, and darted towards her with arms spread wide; the shepherd followed, but not so eagerly.

"My child! my lost darling! my Agnes!" cried the shepherdess.

"Hold them asunder," shouted the king. "Here is more villany! What! have I a scullery-maid in my house born of such parents? The parents of such a child must be capable of any thing. Take all three of them to the rack. Stretch them till their joints are torn asunder, and give them no water. Away with them!"

The soldiers approached to lay hands on them. But, behold! a girl all in rags, with such a radiant countenance that it was right lovely to see, darted between, and careless of the royal presence, flung herself upon the shepherdess, crying,—

"Do not touch her. She is my good, kind mistress."

But the shepherdess could hear or see no one but her Agnes, and pushed her away. Then the princess turned, with the tears in her eyes, to the shepherd, and threw her arms about his neck and pulled down his head and kissed him. And the tall shepherd lifted her to his bosom and kept her there, but his eyes were fixed on his Agnes.

"What is the meaning of this?" cried the king, starting up from his throne. "How did that ragged girl get in here? Take her away with the rest. She is one of them, too."

But the princess made the shepherd set her down, and before any one could interfere she had run up the steps of the dais and then the steps of the king's throne like a squirrel, flung herself upon the king, and begun to smother him with kisses.

All stood astonished, except the three peasants, who did not even see what took place. The shepherdess kept calling to her Agnes, but she was so ashamed that she did not dare even lift her eyes to meet her mother's, and the shepherd kept gazing on her in silence. As for the king, he was so breathless and aghast with astonishment, that he was too feeble to fling the ragged child from him, as he tried to do. But she left him, and running down the steps of the one throne and up those of the other, began kissing the queen next. But the queen cried out,—

"Get away, you great rude child!—Will nobody take her to the rack?"

Then the princess, hardly knowing what she did for joy that she had come in time, ran down the steps of the throne and the dais, and placing herself between the shepherd and shepherdess, took a hand of each, and stood looking at the king and queen.

Their faces began to change. At last they began to know her. But she was so altered—so lovelily altered, that it was no wonder they should not have known her at the first glance; but it was the fault of the pride and anger and injustice with which their hearts were filled, that they did not know her at the second.

The king gazed and the queen gazed, both half risen from their thrones, and looking as if about to tumble down upon her, if only they could be right sure that the ragged girl was their own child. A mistake would be such a dreadful thing!

"My darling!" at last shrieked the mother, a little doubtfully.

"My pet of pets?" cried the father, with an interrogative twist of tone.

Another moment, and they were half way down the steps of the dais.

"Stop!" said a voice of command from somewhere in the hall, and, king and queen as they were, they stopped at once half way, then drew themselves up, stared, and began to grow angry again, but durst not go farther.

The wise woman was coming slowly up through the crowd that filled the hall. Every one made way for her. She came straight on until she stood in front of the king and queen.

"Miserable man and woman!" she said, in words they alone could hear, "I took your daughter away when she was worthy of such parents; I bring her back, and they are unworthy of her. That you did not know her when she came to you is a small wonder, for you have been blind in soul all your lives: now be blind in body until your better eyes are unsealed."

She threw her cloak open. It fell to the ground, and the radiance that flashed from her robe of snowy whiteness, from her face of awful beauty, and from her eyes that shone like pools of sunlight, smote them blind.

Rosamond saw them give a great start, shudder, waver to and fro, then sit down on the steps of the dais; and she knew they were punished, but knew not how. She rushed up to them, and catching a hand of each said—

"Father, dear father! mother dear! I will ask the wise woman to forgive you."

"Oh, I am blind! I am blind!" they cried together. "Dark as night! Stone blind!"

Rosamond left them, sprang down the steps, and kneeling at her feet, cried, "Oh, my lovely wise woman! do let them see. Do open their eyes, dear, good, wise woman."

The wise woman bent down to her, and said, so that none else could hear,

"I will one day. Meanwhile you must be their servant, as I have been yours. Bring them to me, and I will make them welcome."

Rosamond rose, went up the steps again to her father and mother, where they sat like statues with closed eyes, half-way from the top of the dais where stood their empty thrones, seated herself between them, took a hand of each, and was still.

All this time very few in the room saw the wise woman. The moment she threw off her cloak she vanished from the sight of almost all who were present. The woman who swept and dusted the hall and brushed the thrones, saw her, and the shepherd had a glimmering vision of her; but no one else that I know of caught a glimpse of her. The shepherdess did not see her. Nor did Agnes, but she felt her presence upon her like the heat of a furnace seven times heated.

As soon as Rosamond had taken her place between her father and mother, the wise woman lifted her cloak from the floor, and threw it again around her. Then everybody saw her, and Agnes felt as if a soft dewy cloud had come between her and the torrid rays of a vertical sun. The wise woman turned to the shepherd and shepherdess.

"For you," she said, "you are sufficiently punished by the work of your own hands. Instead of making your daughter obey you, you left her to be a slave to herself; you coaxed when you ought to have compelled; you praised when you ought to have been silent; you fondled when you ought to have punished; you threatened when you ought to have inflicted—and there she stands, the full-grown result of your foolishness! She is your crime and your punishment. Take her home with you, and live hour after hour with the pale-hearted disgrace you call your daughter. What she is, the worm at her heart has begun to teach her. When life is no longer endurable, come to me."

"Madam," said the shepherd, "may I not go with you now?"

"You shall," said the wise woman.

"Husband! husband!" cried the shepherdess, "how are we two to get home without you?"

"I will see to that," said the wise woman. "But little of home you will find it until you have come to me. The king carried you hither, and he shall carry you back. But your husband shall not go with you. He cannot now if he would."

The shepherdess looked and saw that the shepherd stood in a deep sleep. She went to him and sought to rouse him, but neither tongue nor hands were of the slightest avail.

The wise woman turned to Rosamond.

"My child," she said, "I shall never be far from you. Come to me when you will. Bring them to me."

Rosamond smiled and kissed her hand, but kept her place by her parents. They also were now in a deep sleep like the shepherd.

The wise woman took the shepherd by the hand, and led him away.

And that is all my double story. How double it is, if you care to know, you must find out. If you think it is not finished—I never knew a story that was. I could tell you a great deal more concerning them all, but I have already told more than is good for those who read but with their foreheads, and enough for those whom it has made look a little solemn, and sigh as they close the book.

Our second tale is one century old. Few stories live to enjoy their centennial, and hence I am happy to be able to include *The Carasoyn* here, in print again for its own birthday.

The story first appeared in MacDonald's *Works of Fancy and Imagination,* which Strahan published in London in 1871. This was a series of ten volumes, incidentally, in which MacDonald reprinted all of his early fantasies, such as the novel *Phantastes,* ghost stories such as *The Portent,* all of the children's fairy-stories he had written up to then, and some other oddities, including the tale that follows.

Like *The Wise Woman,* this next tale bears a certain structural resemblance to the traditional folk-or fairy-tale, but *The Carasoyn* is even less for children. The grim, bleak side of MacDonald's Scots nature, and much of his innate mysticism, come to dominate the tale. Nonetheless, it is frequently lumped together with his shorter fairy-tales, as in the collection *The Light Princess* which Franklin Watts published a few years ago, despite the fact that, at 15,000 words, it is obviously no fairy-tale.

The Carasoyn

I

THE MOUNTAIN STREAM

Once upon a time, there lived in a valley in Scotland, a boy about twelve years of age, the son of a shepherd. His mother was dead, and he had no sister or brother. His father was out all day on the hills with his sheep; but when he came home at night, he was as sure of finding the cottage neat and clean, the floor swept, a bright fire, and his supper waiting for him, as if he had had wife and daughter to look after his household, instead of only a boy. Therefore, although Colin could only read and write, and knew nothing of figures, he was ten times wiser, and more capable of learning anything, than if he had been at school all his days. He was never at a loss when anything had to be done. Somehow, he always blundered into the straight road to his end, while another would be putting on his shoes to look for it. And yet all the time that he was busiest working, he was busiest building castles in the air. I think the two ought always to go together.

And so Colin was never over-worked, but had plenty of time to himself. In winter he spent it in reading by the fireside, or carving pieces of wood with his pocket knife; and in summer he always went out for a ramble. His great delight was in a little stream which ran down the valley from the mountains above. Up this *burn* he would wander every afternoon, with his hands in his pockets. He never got far, however—he was so absorbed in

119

watching its antics. Sometimes he would sit on a rock, staring at the water as it hurried through the stones, scolding, expostulating, muttering, and always having its own way. Sometimes he would stop by a deep pool, and watch the crimson-spotted trouts, darting about as if their thoughts and not their tails sent them where they wanted to go. And when he stopped at the little cascade, tumbling smooth and shining over a hollowed rock, he seldom got beyond it.

But there was one thing which always troubled him. It was, that when the stream came near the cottage, it could find no other way than through the little yard where stood the cowhouse and the pigsty; and there, not finding a suitable channel, spread abroad in a disconsolate manner, becoming rather a puddle than a brook, all defiled with the treading of the cloven feet of the cow and the pigs. In fact, it looked quite lost and ruined; so that even after it had, with much labour, got out of the yard again, it took a long time to gather itself together, and not quite succeeding, slipped away as if ashamed, with spent forces and poverty-stricken speed; till at length, meeting the friendly help of a rivulet coming straight from the hills, it gathered heart and bounded on afresh.

"It can't be all that the cow drinks that makes the difference," said Colin to himself. "The pigs don't care about it. I do believe it's affronted at being dashed about. The cow isn't dirty, but she's rather stupid and inconsiderate. The pigs are dirty. Something must be done. Let me see."

He reconnoitred the whole ground. Upon the other side of the house all was rock, through which he could not cut; and he was forced to the conclusion that the only other course for the stream to take lay right through the cottage.

To most engineers this would have appeared the

one course to be avoided; but Colin's heart danced
at the thought of having his dear *burn* running right
through the house. How cool it would be all the
summer! How convenient for cooking; and how
handy at meals! And then the music of it! How it
would tell him stories, and sing him to sleep at
night! What a companion it would be when his
father was away! And then he could bathe in it
when he liked. In winter—ah!—to be sure. But
winter was a long way off.

The very next day his father went to the fair, so
Colin set to work at once.

It was not such a very difficult undertaking; for
the walls of the cottage, and the floor as well, were
of clay—the former nearly sun-dried into a brick,
and the latter trampled hard; but still both assailable
by pickaxe and spade. He cut through the walls,
and dug a channel along the floor, letting in stones
in the bottom and sides. After it got out of the
cottage and through the small garden in front, it
should find its own way to the channel below, for
here the hill was very steep.

The same evening his father came home.

"What have you been about, Colin?" he asked, in
great surprise, when he saw the trench in the floor.

"Wait a minute, father," said Colin, "till I have
got your supper, and then I'll tell you."

So when his father was seated at the table, Colin
darted out, and hurrying up to the stream, broke
through the bank just in the place whence a natural hollow led straight to the cottage. The stream
dashed out like a wild creature from a cage, faster
than he could follow, and shot through the wall of
the cottage. His father gave a shout; and when Colin
went in, he found him sitting with his spoon half
way to his mouth, and his eyes fixed on the muddy
water which rushed foaming through his floor.

"It will soon be clean, father," said Colin, "and then it will be so nice!"

His father made no answer, but continued staring. Colin went on with a long list of the advantages of having a brook running through your house. At length his father smiled and said:—

"You are a curious creature, Colin. But why shouldn't you have your fancies as well as older people? We'll try it awhile, and then we'll see about it."

The fact was, Colin's father had often thought what a lonely life the boy's was. And it seemed hard to take from him any pleasure he could have. So out rushed Colin at the front, to see how the brook would take the shortest way headlong down the hill to its old channel. And to see it go tumbling down that hill was a sight worth living for.

"It is a mercy," said Colin, "it has no neck to break, or it would break twenty times in a minute. It flings itself from rock to rock right down, just as I should like to do, if it weren't for my neck."

All that evening he was out and in without a moment's rest; now up to the beginning of the cut, now following the stream down to the cottage; then through the cottage, and out again at the front door to see it dart across the garden, and dash itself down the hill.

At length his father told him he must go to bed. He took one more peep at the water, which was running quite clear now, and obeyed. His father followed him presently.

II

THE FAIRY FLEET

The bed was about a couple of yards from the edge of the brook. And as Colin was always first up in the morning, he slept at the front of the bed. So he lay for some time gazing at the faint glimmer of the water in the dull red light from the sod-covered fire, and listening to its sweet music as it hurried through to the night again, till its murmur changed into a lullaby, and sung him fast asleep.

Soon he found that he was coming awake again. He was lying listening to the sound of the busy stream. But it had gathered more sounds since he went to sleep—amongst the rest one of boards knocking together, and a tiny chattering and sweet laughter, like the tinkling of heather-bells. He opened his eyes. The moon was shining along the brook, lighting the smoky rafters above with its reflection from the water, which had been dammed back at its outlet from the cottage, so that it lay bank-full and level with the floor. But its surface was hardly to be seen, save by an occasional glimmer, for the crowded boats of a fairy fleet which had just arrived. The sailors were as busy as sailors could be, mooring along the banks, or running their boats high and dry on the shore. Some had little sails which glimmered white in the moonshine—half-lowered, or blowing out in the light breeze that crept down the course of the stream. Some were pulling about through the rest, oars flashing, tiny

voices calling, tiny feet running, tiny hands hauling
at ropes that ran through blocks of shining ivory.
On the shore stood groups of fairy ladies in all
colours of the rainbow, green predominating, waited
upon by gentlemen all in green, but with red and
yellow feathers in their caps. The queen had landed
on the side next to Colin, and in a few minutes more
twenty dances were going at once along the shores of
the fairy river. And there lay great Colin's face,
just above the bed-clothes, *glowering* at them like
an ogre.

At last, after a few dances, he heard a clear,
sweet, ringing voice say,

"I've had enough of this. I'm tired of doing like
the big people. Let's have a game of Hey
Cockolorum Jig!"

That instant every group sprang asunder, and
every fairy began a frolic on his own account. They
scattered all over the cottage, and Colin lost sight
of most of them.

While he lay watching the antics of two of those
near him, who behaved more like clowns at a fair
than the gentlemen they had been a little while before, he heard a voice close to his ear; but though
he looked everywhere about his pillow, he could
see nothing The voice stopped the moment he began
to look, but began again as soon as he gave it up.

"You can't see me. I'm talking to you through a
hole in the head of your bed."

Colin knew the knot-hole well enough.

"Don't look," said the voice. "If the queen sees
me I shall be pinched. Oh, please don't."

The voice sounded as if its owner would cry
presently. So Colin took good care not to look. It
went on:

"Please, I am a little girl, not a fairy. The queen
stole me the minute I was born, seven years ago,
and I can't get away. I don't like the fairies. They

are so silly. And they never grow any wiser. I grow wiser every year. I want to get back to my own people. They won't let me. They make me play at being somebody else all night long, and sleep all day. That's what they do themselves. And I should so like to be myself. The queen says that's not the way to be happy at all; but I do want very much to be a little girl. Do take me."

"How am I to get you?" asked Colin in a whisper, which sounded, after the sweet voice of the changeling, like the wind in a field of dry beans.

"The queen is so pleased with you that she is sure to offer you something. Choose me. Here she comes."

Immediately he heard another voice, shriller and stronger, in front of him; and, looking about, saw standing on the edge of the bed a lovely little creature, with a crown glittering with jewels, and a rush for a sceptre in her hand, the blossom of which shone like a bunch of garnets.

"You great staring creature!" she said. "Your eyes are much too big to see with. What clumsy hobgoblins you thick folk are!"

So saying, she laid her wand across Colin's eyes.

"Now, then, stupid!" she said; and that instant Colin saw the room like a huge barn, full of creatures about two feet high. The beams overhead were crowded with fairies, playing all imaginable tricks, scrambling everywhere, knocking each other over, throwing dust and soot in each other's faces, grinning from behind corners, dropping on each other's necks, and tripping up each other's heels. Two had got hold of an empty egg-shell, and coming behind one sitting on the edge of the table, and laughing at some one on the floor, tumbled it right over him, so that he was lost in the cavernous hollow. But the lady-fairies mingled in none of these rough pranks.

Their tricks were always graceful, and they had more to say than to do.

But the moment the queen had laid her wand across his eyes, she went on:

"Know, son of a human mortal, that thou hast pleased a queen of the fairies. Lady as I am over the elements, I cannot have everything I desire. One thing thou hast given me. Years have I longed for a path down this rivulet to the ocean below. Your horrid farm-yard, ever since your great grandfather built this cottage, was the one obstacle. For we fairies hate dirt, not only in houses, but in fields and woods as well, and above all in running streams. But I can't talk like this any longer. I tell you what, you are a dear good boy, and you shall have what you please. Ask me for anything you like."

"May it please your majesty," said Colin, very deliberately, "I want a little girl that you carried away some seven years ago the moment she was born. May it please your majesty, I want her."

"It does not please my majesty," cried the queen, whose face had been growing very black. "Ask for something else."

"Then, whether it pleases your majesty or not," said Colin, bravely, "I hold your majesty to your word. I want that little girl, and that little girl I *will* have, and nothing else."

"You dare to talk so to me, you thick!"

"Yes, your majesty."

"Then you shan't have her."

"Then I'll turn the brook right through the dung-hill," said Colin. "Do you think I'll let you come into my cottage to play at high jinks when you please, if you behave to me like this?"

And Colin sat up in bed, and looked the queen in the face. And as he did so he caught sight of the loveliest little creature peeping round the corner at the foot of the bed. And he knew she was the little girl, because she was quiet, and looked frightened, and was sucking her thumb.

Then the queen, seeing with whom she had to deal, and knowing that queens in Fairyland are bound by their word, began to try another plan with him. She put on her sweetest manner and looks; and as she did so, the little face at the foot of the bed grew more troubled, and the little head shook itself, and the little thumb dropped out of the little mouth.

"Dear Colin," said the queen, "you shall have the girl. But you must do something for me first."

The little girl shook her head as fast as ever she could, but Colin was taken up with the queen.

"To be sure I will. What is it?" he said.

And so he was bound by a new bargain, and was in the queen's power.

"You must fetch me a bottle of Carasoyn," said she.

"What is that?" asked Colin.

"A kind of wine that makes people happy."

"Why, are you not happy already?"

"No, Colin," answered the queen, with a sigh.

"You have everything you want."

"Except the Carasoyn," returned the queen.

"You do whatever you like, and go wherever you please."

"That's just it. I want something that I neither like nor please—that I don't know anything about. I want a bottle of Carasoyn."

And here she cried like a spoilt child, not like a sorrowful woman.

"But how am I to get it?"

"I don't know. You must find out."

"Oh! that's not fair," cried Colin.

But the queen burst into a fit of laughter that sounded like the bells of a hundred frolicking sheep, and bounding away to the side of the river, jumped on board of her boat. And like a swarm of bees gathered the courtiers and sailors; two creeping out of the bellows, one at the nozzle and the other at the valve; three out of the basket-hilt of the broadsword on the wall; six all white out of the meal-tub; and so from all parts of the cottage to the river-side. And amongst them Colin spied the little girl creeping on board the queen's boat, with her pinafore to her eyes; and the queen was shaking her fist at her. In five minutes more they had all scrambled into the boats, and the whole fleet was in motion down the stream. In another moment the cottage was empty, and everything had returned to its usual size.

"They'll be all dashed to pieces on the rocks," cried Colin, jumping up, and running into the garden. When he reached the fall, there was nothing to be seen but the swift plunge and rush of the broken water in the moonlight. He thought he heard cries and shouts coming up from below, and fancied he could distinguish the sobs of the little maiden whom he had so foolishly lost. But the sounds might be only those of the water, for to the different voices of a running stream there is no end. He followed its course all the way to its old channel, but saw nothing to indicate any disaster. Then he crept back to his bed, where he lay thinking what a fool he had been, till he cried himself to sleep over the little girl who would never grow into a woman.

III

THE OLD WOMAN AND HER HEN

In the morning, however, his courage had returned; for the word Carasoyn was always saying itself in his brain.

"People in fairy stories," he said, "always find what they want. Why should not I find this Carasoyn? It does not seem likely. But the world doesn't go round by *likely*. So I will try."

But how was he to begin?

When Colin did not know what to do, he always did something. So as soon as his father was gone to the hill, he wandered up the stream down which the fairies had come.

"But I needn't go on so," he said, "for if the Carasoyn grew in the fairies' country, the queen would know how to get it."

All at once he remembered how he had lost himself on the moor when he was a little boy; and had gone into a hut and found there an old woman spinning. And she had told him such stories! and shown him the way home. So he thought she might be able to help him now; for he remembered that she was very old then, and must be older and still wiser now. And he resolved to go and look for the hut, and ask the old woman what he was to do.

So he left the stream, and climbed the hill, and soon came upon a desolate moor. The sun was clouded and the wind was cold, and everything looked dreary. And there was no sign of a hut any-

where. He wandered on, looking for it; and all at
once found that he had forgotten the way back. At
the same instant he saw the hut right before him.
And then he remembered it was when he had lost
himself that he saw it the former time.

"It seems the way to find some things it to lose
yourself," said he to himself.

He went up to the cottage, which was like a large
beehive built of turf, and knocked at the door.

"Come in, Colin," said a voice; and he entered,
stopping low.

The old woman sat by a little fire, spinning, after
the old fashion, with a distaff and spindle. She
stopped the moment he went in.

"Come and sit down by the fire," she said, "and
tell me what you want."

Then Colin saw that she had no eyes.

"I am very sorry you are blind," he said.

"Never you mind that, my dear. I see more than
you do for all my blindness. Tell me what you want,
and I shall see at least what I can do for you."

"How do you know I want anything?" asked
Colin.

"Now that's what I don't like," said the old
woman. "Why do you waste words? Words should
not be wasted any more than crumbs."

"I beg your pardon," returned Colin. "I will tell
you all about it."

And so he told her the whole story.

"Oh those children! those children!" said the old
woman. "They are always doing some mischief.
They never know how to enjoy themselves without
hurting somebody or other. I really must give that
queen a bit of my mind. Well, my dear, I like you;
and I will tell you what must be done. You shall
carry the silly queen her bottle of Carasoyn. But she
won't like it when she gets it, I can tell her. That's
my business, however.—First of all, Colin, you

must dream three days without sleeping. Next, you must work three days without dreaming. And last, you must work and dream three days together."

"How am I to do all that?"

"I will help you all I can, but a great deal will depend on yourself. In the meantime you must have something to eat."

So saying, she rose, and going to a corner behind her bed returned with a large golden-coloured egg in her hand. This she laid on the hearth, and covered over with hot ashes. She then chatted away to Colin about his father, and the sheep and the cow, and the housework, and showed that she knew all about him. At length she drew the ashes off the egg, and put it on a plate.

"It shines like silver now," said Colin.

"That is a sign it is quite done," said she, and set it before him.

Colin had never tasted anything half so nice. And he had never seen such a quantity of meat in an egg. Before he had finished it he had made a hearty meal. But, in the meantime, the old woman said,—

"Shall I tell you a story while you have your dinner?"

"Oh, yes, please do," answered Colin. "You told me such stories before!"

"Jenny," said the old woman, "my wool is all done. Get me some more."

And from behind the bed out came a sober-coloured, but large and beautifully-shaped hen. She walked sedately across the floor, putting down her feet daintily, like a prim matron as she was, and stopping by the door, gave a *cluck, cluck*.

"Oh, the door is shut, is it!" said the old woman.

"Let me open it," said Colin.

"Do, my dear."

"What are all those white things?" he asked, for

the cottage stood in the middle of a great bed of grass with white tops.

"Those are my sheep," said the old woman. "You will see."

Into the grass Jenny walked, and stretching up her neck gathered the white woolly stuff in her beak. When she had as much as she could hold, she came back and dropped it on the floor; then picked the seeds out and swallowed them, and went back for more. The old woman took the wool, and fastening it on her distaff, began to spin, giving the spindle a twirl, and then dropping it and drawing out the thread from the distaff. But as soon as the spindle began to twirl, it began to sparkle all the colours of the rainbow, and it was a delight to see. And the hands of the woman, instead of being old and wrinkled, were young and long-fingered and fair, and they drew out the wool, and the spindle spun and flashed, and the hen kept going out and in, bringing wool and swallowing the seeds, and the old woman kept telling Colin one story after another, till he thought he could sit there all his life and listen. Sometimes it seemed the spindle that was flashing them, sometimes the long fingers that were spinning them, and sometimes the hen that was gathering them off the heads of the long dry grass and bringing them in her beak and laying them down on the floor.

All at once the spindle grew slower, and gradually ceased turning; the fingers stopped drawing out the thread, the hen retreated behind the bed, and the voice of the blind woman was silent.

"I suppose it is time for me to go," said Colin.

"Yes, it is," answered his hostess.

"Please tell me, then, how I am to dream three days without sleeping."

"That's over," said the old woman. "You've

'just finished that part. I told you I would help you all I could."

"Have I been here three days, then?" asked Colin, in astonishment.

"And nights too. And I and Jenny and the spindle are quite tired and want to sleep. Jenny has got three eggs to lay besides. Make haste, my boy."

"Please, then, tell me what I am to do next."

"Jenny will put you in the way. When you come where you are going, you will tell them that the old woman with the spindle desires them to lift Cumberbone Crag a yard higher, and to send a flue under Stonestarvit Moss. Jenny, show Colin the way."

Jenny came out with a surly *cluck,* and led him a good way across the heath by a path only a hen could have found. But she turned suddenly and walked home again.

IV

THE GOBLIN BLACKSMITH

Colin could just perceive something suggestive of a track, which he followed till the sun went down. Then he saw a dim light before him, keeping his eye upon which, he came at last to a smithy, where, looking in at the open door, he saw a huge hump-backed smith working a fore-hammer in each hand.

He grinned out of the middle of his breast when he saw Colin, and said, "Come in; come in: my youngsters will be glad of you."

He was an awful looking creature, with a great hare lip, and a red ball for a nose. Whatever he did —speak, or laugh, or sneeze—he did not stop working one moment. As often as the sparks flew in his face, he snapped at them with his eyes (which were the colour of a half-dead coal), now with this one, now with that: and the more sparks they got into them the brighter his eyes grew. The moment Colin entered, he took a huge bar of iron from the furnace, and began laying on it so with his two fore-hammers that he disappeared in a cloud of sparks, and Colin had to shut his eyes and be glad to escape with a few burns on his face and hands. When he had beaten the iron till it was nearly black, the smith put it in the fire again, and called out a hundred odd names:

"Here Gob, Shag, Latchit, Licker, Freestone, Greywhackit, Mousetrap, Potato-pot, Blob, Blotch, Blunker——"

And ever as he called, one dwarf after another came tumbling out of the chimney in the corner of which the fire was roaring. They crowded about Colin and began to make hideous faces and spit fire at him. But he kept a bold countenance. At length one pinched him, and he could not stand that, but struck him hard on the head. He thought he had knocked his own hand to pieces, it gave him such a jar; and the head rung like an iron pot.

"Come, come, young man?" cried the smith; "you keep your hands off my children."

"Tell them to keep their hands off me, then," said Colin.

And calling to mind his message, just as they began to crowd about him again with yet more spiteful looks, he added—

"Here, you imps! I won't stand it longer. Get to your work directly. The old woman with the spindle says you're to lift Cumberbone Crag a yard higher, and to send a flue under Stonestarvit Moss."

In a moment they had vanished in the chimney. In a moment more the smithy rocked to its foundations. But the smith took no notice, only worked more furiously than ever. Then came a great crack and a shock that threw Colin on the floor. The smith reeled, but never lost hold of his hammers or missed a blow on the anvil.

"Those boys will do themselves a mischief," he said; then turning to Colin, "Here, you sir, take that hammer. This is no safe place for idle people. If you don't work you'll be knocked to pieces in no time."

The same moment there came a wind from the chimney that blew all the fire into the middle of the smithy. The smith dashed up upon the forge, and rushed out of sight. Presently he returned with one of the goblins under his arm kicking and screaming, laid his ugly head down on the anvil, where he held him by the neck, and hit him a great blow with his hammer above the ear. The hammer rebounded, the goblin gave a shriek, and the smith flung him into the chimney, saying—

"That's the only way to serve *him.* You'll be more careful for one while, I guess, Slobberkin."

And thereupon he took up his other hammer and began to work again, saying to Colin,

"Now, young man, as long as you get a blow with your hammer in for every one of mine, you'll be quite safe; but if you stop, or lose the beat, I won't be answerable to the old woman with the spindle for the consequences."

Colin took up his hammer and did his best. But he soon found that he had never known what it was to work. The smith worked a hammer in each hand, and it was all Colin could do to work his little hammer with both his hands; so it was a terrible exertion to put in blow for blow with the smith. Once, when he lost the time, the smith's fore-hammer came down on the head of his, beat it flat on the anvil, and flung the handle to the other end of the smithy, where it struck the wall like the report of a cannon.

"I told you," said the smith. "There's another. Make haste, for the boys will be in want of you and me too before they get Cumberbone Crag half a foot higher."

Presently in came the biggest-headed of the family, out of the chimney.

"Six-foot wedges, and a three-yard crowbar!" he said; "or Cumberbone will cumber our bones presently."

The smith rushed behind the bellows, brought out a bar of iron three inches thick or so, cut off three yards, put the end in the fire, blew with might and main, and brought it out as white as paper. He and Colin then laid upon it till the end was flattened to an edge, which the smith turned up a little. He then handed the tool to the imp.

"Here, Gob," he said, "run with it, and the wedges will be ready by the time you come back."

Then to the wedges they set. And Colin worked like three. He never knew how he could work before. Not a moment's pause, except when the smith was at the forge for another glowing mass! And yet, to Colin's amazement, the more he worked, the stronger he seemed to grow. Instead of being worn out, the moment he had got his breath he wanted to be at it again; and he felt as if he had grown twice the size since he took hammer in hand. And the goblins kept running in and out all the time, now for one thing, now for another. Colin thought if they made use of all the tools they fetched, they must be working very hard indeed. And the convulsions felt in the smithy bore witness to their exertions somewhere in the neighbourhood.

And the longer they worked together, the more friendly grew the smith. At length he said—his words always adding energy to his blows—

"What does the old woman want to improve Stonestarvit Moss for?"

"I didn't know she did want to improve it," returned Colin.

"Why, anybody may see that. First, she wants Cumberbone Crag a yard higher—just enough to send the north-east blast over the Moss without touching it. Then she wants a hot flue passed under it. Plain as a fore-hammer!—What did you ask her to do for you? She's always doing things for people and making my bones ache."

"You don't seem to mind it much, though, sir," said Colin.

"No more I do," answered the smith, with a blow that drove the anvil half way into the earth, from which it took him some trouble to drag it out again. "But I want to know what she is after now."

So Colin told him all he knew about it, which was merely his own story.

"I see, I see," said the smith. "It's all moonshine; but we must do as she says notwithstanding. And now it is my turn to give you a lift, for you have worked well.—As soon as you leave the smithy, go straight to Stonestarvit Moss. Get on the highest part of it; make a circle three yards across, and dig a trench round it. I will give you a spade. At the end of the first day you will see a vine break the earth. By the end of the second, it will be creeping all over the circle. And by the end of the third day, the grapes will be ripe. Squeeze them one by one into a bottle—I will give you a bottle—till it is full. Cork it up tight, and by the time the queen comes for it, it will be Carasoyn."

"Oh, thank you, thank you," cried Colin. "When am I to go?"

"As soon as the boys have lifted Cumberbone Crag, and bored the flue under the Moss. It is of no use till then."

"Well, I'll go on with my work," said Colin, and struck away at the anvil.

In a minute or two in came the same goblin whose head his father had hammered, and said, respectfully.

"It's all right, sir. The boys are gathering their tools, and will be home to supper directly."

"Are you sure you have lifted the Crag a yard?" said the smith.

"Slumkin says it's a half inch over the yard. Grungle says it's three-quarters. But that won't matter—will it?"

"No. I dare say not. But it is much better to be accurate. Is the flue done?"

"Yes, we managed that partly in lifting the crag."

"Very well. How's your head?"

"It rings a little."

"Let it ring you a lesson, then, Slobberkin, in future."

"Yes, sir."

"Now, master, you may go when you like," said the smith to Colin. "We've nothing here you can eat, I am sorry to say."

"Oh, I don't mind that. I'm not very hungry. But the old woman with the spindle said I was to work three days without dreaming."

"Well, you haven't been dreaming—have you?"

And the smith looked quite furious as he put the question, lifting his fore-hammer as if he would serve Colin like Slobberkin.

"No, that I haven't," answered Colin. "You took good care of that, sir."

The smith actually smiled.

"Then go along," he said. "It is all right."

"But I've only worked——"

"Three whole days and nights," interrupted the smith. "Get along with you. The boys will bother you if you don't. Here's your spade and here's your bottle."

V

THE MOSS VINEYARD

Colin did not need a hint more, but was out of
the smithy in a moment. He turned, however, to ask
the way: there was nothing in sight but a great heap
of peats which had been dug out of the moss, and
was standing there to dry. Could he be on Stonestarvit Moss already? The sun was just setting. He
would look out for the highest point at once. So he
kept climbing, and at last reached a spot whence he
could see all round him for a long way. Surely that
must be Cumberbone Crag looking down on him!
And there at his feet lay one of Jenny's eggs, as
bright as silver. And there was a little path trodden
and scratched by Jenny's feet, enclosing a circle just
the size the smith had told him to make. He set to
work at once, ate Jenny's egg, and then dug the
trench.

Those three days were the happiest he had ever
known. For he understood everything he did himself, and all that everything was doing round about
him. He saw what the rushes were, and why the
blossom came out at the side, and why it was
russet-coloured, and why the pith was white, and
the skin green. And he said to himself, "If I were a
rush now, that's just how I should make a point of
growing." And he knew how the heather felt with
its cold roots, and its head of purple bells; and the
wise-looking cotton-grass, which the old woman
called her sheep, and the white beard of which she

spun into thread. And he knew what she spun it
for: namely, to weave it into lovely white cloth of
which to make nightgowns for all the good people
that were like to die; for one with one of these
nightgowns upon him never died, but was laid in a
beautiful white bed, and the door was closed upon
him, and no noise came near him, and he lay
there, dreaming lovely cool dreams, till the world
had turned round, and was ready for him to get up
again and do something.

He felt the wind playing with every blade of grass
in his charmed circle. He felt the rays of heat shooting up from the hot flue beneath the moss. He knew
the moment when the vine was going to break from
the earth, and he felt the juices gathering and
flowing from the roots into the grapes. And all the
time he seemed at home, tending the cow, or making his father's supper, or reading a fairy tale as he
sat waiting for him to come home.

At length the evening of the third day arrived.
Colin squeezed the rich red grapes into his bottle,
corked it, shouldered his spade, and turned home-
wards, guided by a peak which he knew in the
distance. After walking all night in the moonlight,
he came at length upon a place which he recognized, and so down upon the brook, which he
followed home.

He met his father going out with his sheep. Great
was his delight to see Colin again, for he had been
dreadfully anxious about him. Colin told him the
whole story; and as at that time marvels were much
easier to believe than they are now, Colin's father
did not laugh at him, but went away to the hills
thinking, while Colin went on to the cottage, where
he found plenty to do, having been nine days gone.
He laid the bottle carefully away with his Sunday
clothes, and set about everything just as usual.

But though the fairy brook was running merrily

as ever through the cottage, and although Colin watched late every night, and latest when the moon shone, no fairy fleet came glimmering and dancing in along the stream. Autumn was there at length, and cold fogs began to rise in the cottage, and so Colin turned the brook into its old course, and filled up the breaches in the walls and the channel along the floor, making all close against the blasts of winter. But he had never known such a weary winter before. He could not help constantly thinking how cold the little girl must be, and how she would be saying to herself, "I wish Colin hadn't been so silly and lost me."

VI

THE CONSEQUENCES

But at last the spring came, and after the spring the summer. And the very first warm day, Colin took his spade and pickaxe, and down rushed the stream once more, singing and bounding into the cottage. Colin was even more delighted than he had been the first time. And he watched late into the night, but there came neither moon nor fairy fleet. And more than a week passed thus.

At length, on the ninth night, Colin, who had just fallen asleep, opened his eyes with sudden wakefulness, and behold! the room was all in a glimmer with moonshine and fairy glitter. The boats were rocking on the water, and the queen and her court had landed, and were dancing merrily on the earthen floor. He lost no time.

"Queen! queen!" he said, "I've got your bottle of Carasoyn."

The dance ceased in a moment, and the queen bounded upon the edge of his bed.

"I can't bear the look of your great, glaring, ugly eyes," she said. "I must make you less before I can talk to you."

So once more she laid her rush wand across his eyes, whereupon Colin saw them all six times the size they were before, and the queen went on:

"Where is the Carasoyn? Give it me."

"It is in my box under the bed. If your majesty will stand out of the way, I will get it for you."

The queen jumped on the floor, and Colin, leaning from the bed, pulled out his little box, and got out the bottle.

"There it is, your majesty," he said, but not offering it to her.

"Give it me directly," said the queen, holding out her hand.

"First give me my little girl," returned Colin, boldly.

"Do you dare to bargain with me?" said the queen, angrily.

"Your majesty deigned to bargain with me first," said Colin.

"But since then you tried to break all our necks. You made a wicked cataract out there on the other side of the garden. Our boats were all dashed to pieces, and we had to wait till our horses were fetched. If I had been killed, you couldn't have held me to my bargain, and I won't hold to it now."

"If you chose to go down my cataract——" began Colin.

"*Your* cataract!" cried the queen. "All the waters that run from Loch Lonely are mine, I can tell you —all the way to the sea."

"Except where they run through farmyards, your majesty."

"I'll rout you out of the country," said the queen.

"Meantime I'll put the bottle in the chest again," returned Colin.

The queen bit her lips with vexation.

"Come here, Changeling," she cried at length, in a flattering tone.

And the little girl came slowly up to her, and stood staring at Colin, with the tears in her eyes.

"Give me your hand, little girl," said he, holding out his.

She did so. It was cold as ice.

"Let go her hand," said the queen.

"I won't," said Colin. "She's mine."

"Give me the bottle then," said the queen.

"Don't," said the child.

But it was too late. The queen had it.

"Keep your girl," she cried, with an ugly laugh.

"Yes, keep me," cried the child.

The cry ended in a hiss.

Colin felt something slimy wriggling in his grasp, and looking down, saw that instead of a little girl he was holding a great writhing worm. He had almost flung it from him, but recovering himself, he grasped it tighter.

"If it's a snake, I'll choke it," he said. "If it's a girl, I'll keep her."

The same instant it changed to a little white rabbit, which looked him piteously in the face, and pulled to get its little forefoot out of his hand. But, though he tried not to hurt it, Colin would not let it go. Then the rabbit changed to a great black cat, with eyes that flashed green fire. She sputtered and spit and swelled her tail, but all to no purpose. Colin held fast. Then it was a wood pigeon, struggling and fluttering in terror to get its wing out of his hold. But Colin still held fast.

All this time the queen had been getting the cork out. The moment it yielded she gave a scream and dropped the bottle. The Carasoyn ran out, and a strange odour filled the cottage. The queen stood shivering and sobbing beside the bottle, and all her court came about her and shivered and sobbed too, and their faces grew ancient and wrinkled. Then the queen, bending and tottering like an old woman, led the way to the boats, and her courtiers followed her, limping and creeping and distorted. Colin stared in amazement. He saw them all go aboard, and he heard the sound of them like a far-off company of men and women crying bitterly. And away they floated down the stream, the rowers dipping no oar, but bending weeping over them, and letting the boats drift along the stream. They vanished from his sight, and the rush of the cataract came up on the night-wind louder than he had ever heard it before.—But alas! when he came to himself, he found his hand relaxed, and the dove flown. Once more there was nothing left but to cry himself asleep, as he well might.

In the morning he rose very wretched. But the moment he entered the cowhouse, there, beside the cow, on the milking stool, sat a lovely little girl, with just one white garment on her, crying bitterly.

"I am so cold," she said, sobbing.

He caught her up, ran with her into the house, put her into the bed, and ran back to the cow for a bowl of warm milk. This she drank eagerly, laid her head down, and fell fast asleep. Then Colin saw that though she must be eight years old by her own account, her face was scarcely older than that of a baby of as many months.

When his father came home you may be sure he stared to see the child in the bed. Colin told him what had happened. But his father said he had met a troop of gipsies on the hill that morning.

"And you were always a dreamer, Colin, even before you could speak."

"But don't you smell the Carasoyn still?" said Colin.

"I do smell something very pleasant, to be sure," returned his father; "but I think it is the wallflower on the top of the garden-wall. What a blossom there is of it this year! I am sure there is nothing sweeter in all Fairyland, Colin."

Colin allowed that.

The little girl slept for three whole days. And for three days more she never said another word than,

"I am so cold!" But after that she began to revive a little, and to take notice of things about her. For three weeks she would taste nothing but milk warm from the cow, and would not move from the chimney-corner. By degrees, however, she began to help Colin a little with his house-work, and as she did so, her face gathered more and more expression; and she made such progress, that by the end of three months she could do everything as well as Colin himself, and certainly more neatly. Whereupon he gave up his duties to her, and went out with his father to learn the calling of a shepherd.

Thus things went on for three years. And Fairy, as they called her, grew lovelier every day, and looked up to Colin more and more every day.

At the end of the three years, his father sent him to an old friend of his, a schoolmaster. Before he left, he made Fairy promise never to go near the brook after sundown. He had turned it into its old channel the very day she came to them. And he begged his father especially to look after her when the moon was high, for then she grew very restless and strange, and her eyes looked as if she saw things other people could not see.

When the end of the other three years had come, the schoolmaster would not let Colin go home, but insisted on sending him to college. And there he remained for three years more.

When he returned at the end of that time, he found Fairy so beautiful and so wise, that he fell dreadfully in love with her. And Fairy found out that she had been in love with him since ever so long—she did not know how long. And Colin's father agreed that they should be married as soon as Colin should have a house to take her to. So Colin went away to London, and worked very hard, till at last he managed to get a little cottage in

Devonshire to live in. Then he went back to Scotland and married Fairy. And he was very glad to get her away from the neighbourhood of a queen who was not to be depended upon.

VII

THE BANISHED FAIRIES

Those fairies had for a long time been doing wicked things. They had played many ill-natured pranks upon the human mortals; had stolen children upon whom they had no claim; had refused to deliver them up when they were demanded of them; had even terrified infants in their cradles; and, final proof of moral declension in fairies, had attempted to get rid of the obligations of their word, by all kinds of trickery and false logic.

It was not till they had sunk thus low that their queen began to long for the Carasoyn. She, no more than if she had been a daughter of Adam, could be happy while going on in that way; and, therefore, having heard of its marvellous virtues, and thinking it would stop her growing misery, she tried hard to procure it. For a hundred years she had tried in vain. Not till Colin arose did she succeed. But the Carasoyn was only for really good people, and therefore when the iron bottle which contained it was uncorked, she, and all her attendants were, by the vapours thereof, suddenly changed into old men and women fairies. They crowded away weeping and lamenting, and Colin had as yet seen them no more.

For when the wickedness of any fairy tribe reaches its climax, the punishment that falls upon them is, that they are compelled to leave that part of the country where they and their ancestors have lived for more years than they can count, and wander away, driven by an inward restlessness, ever longing after the country they have left, but never able to turn round and go back to it, always thinking they will do so to-morrow, but when to-morrow comes, saying *to-morrow* again, till at last they find, not their old home, but the place of their doom— that is, a place where their restlessness leaves them, and they find they can remain. This partial repose, however, springs from no satisfaction with the place; it is only that their inward doom ceases to drive them further. They sit down to weep, and to long after the country they have left.

This is not because the country to which they have been driven is ugly and inclement—it may or may not be such; it is simply because it is not *their* country. If it would be, and it must be, torture to the fairy of a harebell to go and live in a hyacinth— a torture quite analogous to which many human beings undergo from their birth to their death, and some of them longer, for anything I can tell—think what it must be for a tribe of fairies to have to go and live in a country quite different from that in and for which they were born. To the whole tribe the country is what the flower is to the individual; and when a fairy is born to whom the whole country is what the individual flower is to the individual fairy, then the fairy is king or queen of the fairies, and always makes a new nursery rhyme for the young fairies, which is never forgotten. When, therefore, a tribe is banished, it is long before they can settle themselves into their new quarters. Their clothes do not fit them, as it were. They are constantly wriggling themselves into harmony with their new circumstances—which is only another word for clothes—and never quite succeeding. It is their punishment—and something more. Consequently their temper is not always of the evenest; indeed, and in a word, they are as like human mortals as may well be, considering the differences between them.

In the present case, you would say it was surely no great hardship to be banished from the heathy hills, the bare rocks, the wee trotting burnies of Scotland, to the rich valleys, the wooded shores, the great rivers, the grand ocean of the south of Devon. You may say they could not have been very wicked when this was all their punishment. If you do, you must have studied the human mortals to no great purpose. You do not believe that a man may be punished by being made very rich? I do. Anyhow, these fairies were not of your opinion, *for they were in it.* In the splendour of their Devon banishment, they sighed for their bare Scotland. Under the leafy foliage of the Devonshire valleys, with the purple and green ocean before them, that had seen ships of a thousand builds, or on the shore rich with shells and many-coloured creatures, they longed for the clear, cold, pensive, open sides of the far-stretching heathy sweeps to which a grey, wild, torn sea, with memories only of Norsemen, whales, and mermaids, cried aloud. For the big rivers, on which reposed great old hulks scarred with battle, they longed after the rocks and stones and rowan and birch trees of the solitary burns. The country they had left might be an ill-favoured thing, but it was their own.

Now that which happens to the aspect of a country when the fairies leave it, is that a kind of deadness falls over the landscape. The traveller feels the wind as before, but it does not seem to refresh him. The child sighs over his daisy chain, and cannot find a red-tipped one amongst all that he has gathered. The cowslips have not half the honey in them. The wasps outnumber the bees. The horses come from the plough more tired at night, hanging

their heads to their very hoofs as they plod home-
wards. The youth and the maiden, though perfectly
happy when they meet, find the road to and from
the trysting-place unaccountably long and dreary.
The hawthorn-blossom is neither so white nor so
red as it used to be, and the dark rough bark looks
through and makes it ragged. The day is neither so
warm nor the night so friendly as before. In a word,
that something which no one can either describe or
be content to go without is missing. Everything is
common-place. Everything falls short of one's expec-
tations.

But it does not follow that the country to which
the fairies are banished is so much richer and more
beautiful for their presence. If that country has its
own fairies, it needs no more, and Devon in especial
has been rich in fairies from the time of the Phoe-
nicians, and ever so long before that. But supposing
there were no aborigines left to quarrel with, it
takes centuries before the new immigration can fit
itself into its new home. Until this comes about, the
queerest things are constantly happening. For however could a convolvulus grow right with the soul of
a Canterbury-bell inside it, for instance? The banished fairies are forced to do the best they can,
and take the flowers the nearest they can find.

VIII

THEIR REVENGE

When Colin and his wife settled then in their farmhouse, the same tribe of fairies was already in the neighbourhood, and was not long in discovering who had come after them. An assembly was immediately called. Something must be done; but what, was disputed. Most of them thought only of revenge—to be taken upon the children. But the queen hesitated. Perhaps her sufferings had done her good. She suggested that before coming to any conclusion they should wait and watch the household.

In consequence of this resolution they began to frequent the house constantly, and sometimes in great numbers. But for a long time they could do the children no mischief. Whatever they tried turned out to their amusement. They were three, two girls and a boy; the girls nine and eight, and the boy three years old.

When they succeeded in enticing them beyond the home-boundaries, they would at one time be seized with an unaccountable panic, and turn and scurry home without knowing why; at another, a great butterfly or dragon fly, or some other winged and lovely creature, would dart past them, and away towards the house, and they after it, scampering; or the voice of their mother would be heard calling from the door. But at last their opportunity arrived.

One day the children were having such a game!

The sisters had blindfolded their little brother, and were carrying him now on their backs, now in their arms, all about the place; now up stairs, talking about the rugged mountain paths they were climbing; now down again, filling him with the fancy that they were descending into a narrow valley; then they would set the tap of a rain-water barrel running, and represent that they were travelling along the bank of a rivulet. Now they were threading the depths of a great forest: and when the low of a cow reached them from a nigh field, that was the roaring of a lion or a tiger. At length they reached a lake into which the rivulet ran, and then it was necessary to take off his shoes and socks, that he might skim over the water on his bare feet, which they dipped and dabbled now in this tub, now in that, standing for farm and household purposes by the water-butt. The sisters kept their own imaginations alive by carrying him through all the strange places inside and outside of the house. When they told him they were ascending a precipice, they were, in fact, climbing a rather difficult ladder up to the door of the hay-loft; when they told him they were traversing a pathless desert, they were, in fact, in a waste, empty place, a wide floor, used sometimes as a granary, with the rafters of the roof coming down to it on both sides, a place abundantly potent in their feelings to the generation of the desert in his; when they were wandering through a trackless forest, they were, in fact, winding about amongst the trees of a large orchard, which, in the moonlight, was vast enough for the fancy of any child. Had they uncovered his eyes at any moment, he would only have been seized with a wonder and awe of another sort, more overwhelming because more real, and more strange because not even in part bodied forth from his own brain.

In the course of the story, and while they bore the

bare-footed child through the orchard, telling him they saw the fairies gliding about everywhere through the trees, not thinking that he believed every word they told him, they set him down, and the child suddenly opened his eyes. His sisters were gone. The moon was staring at him out of the sky, through the mossy branches of the apple-trees, which he thought looked like old women all about him, they were so thin and bony.

When the sisters, who had only for a moment run behind some of the trees, that they might cause him additional amazement, returned, he was gone. There was terrible lamentation in the house; but his father and mother, who were experienced in such matters, knew that the fairies must be in it, and cherished a hope that their son would yet be restored to them, though all their endeavours to find him were unavailing.

IX

THE FAIRY FIDDLER

The father thought over many plans, but never came upon the right one. He did not know that they were the same tribe which had before carried away his wife when she was an infant. If he had, they might have done something sooner.

At length, one night, towards the close of seven years, about twelve o'clock, Colin suddenly opened his eyes, for he had been fast asleep and dreaming, and saw a few grotesque figures which he thought he must have seen before, dancing on the floor between him and the nearly extinguished fire. One of them had a violin, but when Colin first saw him he was not playing. Another of them was singing, and thus keeping the dance in time. This was what he sang, evidently addressed to the fiddler, who stood in the centre of the dance:—

"Peterkin, Peterkin, tall and thin,
  What have you done with his cheek and his chin?
  What have you done with his ear and his eye?
  Hearken, hearken, and hear him cry."

Here Peterkin put his fiddle to his neck, and drew from it a wail just like the cry of a child, at which the dancers danced more furiously. Then he went on playing the tune the other had just sung, in accompaniment to his own reply:—

"Silversnout, Silversnout, short and stout,
I have cut them off and plucked them out,
And salted them down in the Kelpie's Pool,
Because papa Colin is such a fool."

Then the fiddle cried like a child again, and they
danced more wildly than ever.

Colin, filled with horror, although he did not
more than half believe what they were saying, sat
up in bed and stared at them with fierce eyes, waiting to hear what they would say next. Silversnout
now resumed his part:—

"Ho, ho! Ho! ho! and if he don't know,
And fish them out of the pool, so—so,—"

here they all pretended to be hauling in a net as
they danced.

"Before the end of seven long years,
Sweet babe will be left without eyes or ears."

Then Peterkin replied:—

"Sweet babe will be left without cheek or chin,
Only a hole to put porridge in;
Porridge and milk, and haggis, and cakes:
Sweet babe will gobble till his stomach aches."

From this last verse, Colin knew that they must be
Scotch fairies, and all at once recollected their
figures as belonging to the multitude he had once
seen frolicking in his father's cottage. It was now
Silversnout's turn. He began:—

"But never more shall Colin see
Sweet babe again upon his knee,

With or without his cheek or chin,
Except——"

Here Silversnout caught sight of Colin's face staring at him from the bed, and with a shriek of laughter they all vanished, the tones of Peterkin's fiddle trailing after them through the darkness like the train of a shooting star.

X

THE OLD WOMAN AND HER HEN

Now Colin had got the better of these fairies once, not by his own skill, but by the help that other powers had afforded him. What were those powers? First the old woman on the heath. Indeed, he might attribute it all to her. He would go back to Scotland and look for her and find her. But the old woman was never found except by the seeker losing himself. It could not be done otherwise. She would cease to be the old woman, and become her own hen, if ever the moment arrived when any one found her without losing himself. And Colin since that time had wandered so much all over the moor, wide as it was, that lay above his father's cottage, that he did not believe he was able to lose himself there any more. He had yet to learn that it did not so much matter where he lost himself, provided only he was lost.

Just at this time Colin's purse was nearly empty, and he set out to borrow the money of a friend who lived on the other side of Dartmoor. When he got there, he found that he had gone from home. Unable to rest, he set out again to return.

It was almost night when he started, and before he had got many miles into the moor, it was dark, for there was no moon, and it was so cloudy that he could not see the stars. He thought he knew the way quite well, but as the track even in daylight was in certain places very indistinct, it was no wonder that he strayed from it, and found that he had lost himself. The same moment that he became aware of this, he saw a light away to the left. He turned towards it and found it proceeded from a little hive-like hut, the door of which stood open. When he was within a yard or two of it, he heard a voice say—

"Come in, Colin; I'm waiting for you."

Colin obeyed at once, and found the old woman seated with her spindle and distaff, just as he had seen her when he was a boy on the moor above his father's cottage.

"How do you do, mother?" he said.

"I am always quite well. Never ask me that question."

"Well, then, I won't any more," returned Colin. "But I thought you lived in Scotland?"

"I don't live anywhere; but those that will do as I tell them, will always find me when they want me."

"Do you see yet, mother?"

"See! I always see so well that it is not worth while to burn eyelight. So I let them go out. They were expensive."

Where her eyes should have been, there was nothing but wrinkles.

"What do you want?" she resumed.

"I want my child. The fairies have got him."

"I know that."

"And they have taken out his eyes."

"I can make him see without them."

"And they've cut off his ears," said Colin.

"He can hear without them."

"And they've salted down his cheek and his chin."

"Now I don't believe that," said the old woman.

"I heard them say so myself," returned Colin.

"Those fairies are worse liars than any I know. But something must be done. Sit down and I'll tell you a story."

"There's only nine days of the seven years left," said Colin, in a tone of expostulation.

"I know that as well as you," answered the old woman. "Therefore, I say, there is no time to be lost. Sit down and listen to my story. Here, Jenny."

The hen came pacing solemnly out from under the bed.

"Off to the sheep-shearing, Jenny, and make haste, for I must spin faster than usual. There are but nine days left."

Jenny ran out at the door with her head on a level with her tail, as if the kite had been after her. In a few moments she returned with a bunch of wool, as they called it, though it was only cotton from the cotton-grass that grew all about the cottage, nearly as big as herself, in her bill, and then darted away for more. The old woman fastened it on her distaff, drew out a thread to her spindle, and then began to spin. And as she spun she told her story—fast, fast; and Jenny kept scampering out and in; and by the time Colin thought it must be midnight, the story was told, and seven of the nine days were over.

"Colin," said the old woman, "now that you know all about it, you must set off at once."

"I am ready," answered Colin, rising.

"Keep on the road Jenny will show you till you come to the cobbler's. Tell him the old woman with the distaff requests him to give you a lump of his wax."

"And what am I to do with it?"

"The cobbler always knows what his wax is for."

And with this answer, the old woman turned her face towards the fire, for, although it was summer, it was cold at night on the moor. Colin, moved by sudden curiosity, instead of walking out of the hut after Jenny, as he ought to have done, crept round by the wall, and peeped in the old woman's face.

There, instead of wrinkled blindness, he saw a pair of flashing orbs of light, which were rather reflected on the fire than had the fire reflected in them. But the same instant the hut and all that was in it vanished, he felt the cold fog of the moor blowing upon him, and fell heavily to the earth.

XI

THE GOBLIN COBBLER

When he came to himself he lay on the moor still. He got up and gazed around. The moon was up, but there was no hut to be seen. He was sorry enough now that he had been so foolish. He called, "Jenny, Jenny," but in vain. What was he to do? To-morrow was the eighth of the nine days left, and if before twelve at night the following day he had not rescued his boy, nothing could be done, at least for seven years more. True, the year was not quite out till about seven the following evening, but the fairies instead of giving days of grace, always take them. He could do nothing but begin to walk, simply because that gave him a shadow more of a chance of finding the cobbler's than if he sat still, but there was no possibility of choosing one direction rather than another.

He wandered the rest of that night and the next day. He could not go home before the hour when the cobbler could no longer help him. Such was his anxiety, that although he neither ate nor drank, he never thought of the cause of his gathering weakness.

As it grew dark, however, he became painfully aware of it, and was just on the point of sitting down exhausted upon a great white stone that looked inviting, when he saw a faint glimmering in front of him. He was erect in a moment, and making towards the place. As he drew near he became aware of a noise made up of many smaller noises, such as might have proceeded from some kind of factory. Not till he was close to the place could he see that it was a long low hut, with one door, and no windows. The light shone from the door, which stood wide open. He approached, and peeped in. There sat a multitude of cobblers, each on his stool, with his candle stuck in the hole in the seat, cobbling away. They looked rather little men, though not at all of fairy-size. The most remarkable thing about them was, that at any given moment they were all doing precisely the same thing, as if they had been a piece of machinery. When one drew the threads in stitching, they all did the same. If Colin saw one wax his thread, and looked up, he saw that they were all waxing their thread. If one took to hammering on his lapstone, they did not follow his example, but all together with him they caught up their lapstones and fell to hammering away, as if nothing but hammering could ever be demanded of them. And when he came to look at them more closely, he saw that every one was blind of an eye, and had a nose turned up like an awl. Every one of them, however, looked different from the rest, notwithstanding a very close resemblance in their features.

The moment they caught sight of him, they rose as one man, pointed their awls at him and advanced towards him like a closing bush of aloes, glittering with spikes.

"Fine upper-leathers," said one and all, with a variety of accordant grimaces.

"Top of his head—good paste-bowl," was the next general remark.

"Coarse hair—good ends," followed.

"Sinews—good thread."

"Bones and blood—good paste for seven-leaguers."

"Ears—good loops to pull 'em on with. Pair short now."

"Soles—same for queen's slippers."

And so on they went, portioning out his body in the most irreverent fashion for the uses of their trade, till having come to his teeth, and said—

"Teeth—good brads,"—they all gave a shriek like the whisk of the waxed threads through the leather, and sprung upon him with their awls drawn back like daggers. There was no time to lose.

"The old woman with the spindle——" said Colin.

"Don't know her," shrieked the cobblers.

"The old woman with the distaff," said Colin, and they all scurried back to their seats and fell to hammering vigorously.

"She desired me," continued Colin, "to ask the cobbler for a lump of his wax."

Every one of them caught up his lump of rosin, and held it out to Colin. He took the one offered by the nearest, and found that all their lumps were gone; after which they sat motionless and stared at him.

"But what am I to do with it?" asked Colin.

"I will walk a little way with you," said the one nearest, "and tell you all about it. The old woman is my grandmother, and a very worthy old soul she is."

Colin stepped out at the door of the workshop, and the cobbler followed him. Looking round, Colin saw all the stools vacant, and the place as still as an old churchyard. The cobbler, who now in his talk, gestures, and general demeanour, appeared a very respectable, not to say conventional, little man, proceeded to give him all the information he required, accompanying it with the present of one of his favourite awls.

They walked a long way, till Colin was amazed to find that his strength stood out so well. But at length the cobbler said—

"I see, sir, that the sun is at hand. I must return to my vocation. When the sun is once up you will know where you are."

He turned aside a few yards from the path, and entered the open door of a cottage. In a moment the place resounded with the soft hammering of three hundred and thirteen cobblers, each with his candle stuck in a hole in the stool on which he sat. While Colin stood gazing in wonderment, the rim of the sun crept up above the horizon; and there the cottage stood white and sleeping, while the cobblers, their lights, their stools, and their tools had all vanished. Only there was still the sound of the hammers ringing in his head, where it seemed to shape itself into words something like these: a good deal had to give way to the rhyme, for they were more particular about their rhymes than their etymology:

> Dub-a-dub, dub-a-dub,
> Cobbler's man
> Hammer it, stitch it,
> As fast as you can.
> The week-day ogre
> Is wanting his boots;
> The trip-a-trap fairy
> Is going bare-foots.
> Dream-daughter has worn out
> Her heels and her toeses,
> For want of cork slippers
> To walk over noses.
> Spark-eye, the smith,
> May shoe the nightmare,
> The kelpie and pookie,
> The nine-footed bear:
> We shoe the mermaids—
> The tips of their tails—
> Stitching the leather

On to their scales.
We shoe the brownie,
Clumsy and toeless,
And then he goes quiet
As a mole or a moless.
There is but one creature
That we cannot shoe,
And that is the Boneless,
All made of glue.

A great deal of nonsense of this sort went through Colin's head before the sounds died away. Then he found himself standing in the field outside his own orchard.

XII

THE WAX AND THE AWL

The evening arrived. The sun was going down over the sea, cloudless, casting gold from him lavishly, when Colin arrived on the shore at some distance from his home. The tide was falling, and a good space of sand was uncovered, and lay glittering in the setting sun. This sand lay between some rocks and the sea; and from the rocks innumerable runnels of water that had been left behind in their hollows were hurrying back to their mother. These occasionally spread into little shallow lakes, resting in hollows in the sand. These lakes were in a constant ripple from the flow of the little streams through them; and the sun shining on these multitudinous ripples, the sand at the bottom shone like brown silk watered with gold, only that the golden lines were flitting about like living things, never for a moment in one place.

Now Colin had no need of fairy ointment to anoint his eyes and make him able to see fairies. Most people need this; but Colin was naturally gifted. Therefore, as he drew near a certain high rock, which he knew very well, and from which many streams were flowing back into the sea, he saw that the little lakes about it were crowded with fairies, playing all kinds of pranks in the water. It was a lovely sight to see them thus frolicking in the light of the setting sun, in their gay dresses, sparkling with jewels, or what looked like jewels, flashing all colours as they moved. But Colin had not much time to see them; for the moment they saw him, knowing that this was the man whom they had wronged by stealing his child, and knowing too that he saw them, they fled at once up the high rock and vanished. This was just what Colin wanted. He went all round and round the rock, looked in every direction in which there might be a pool, found more fairies, here and there, who fled like the first up the rock and disappeared. When he had thus driven them all from the sands, he approached the rock, taking the lump of cobbler's wax from his pocket as he went. He scrambled up the rock, and, without showing his face, put his hand on the uppermost edge of it, and began drawing a line with the wax all along. He went creeping round the rock, still drawing the wax along the edge, till he had completed the circuit. Then he peeped over.

Now in the heart of this rock, which was nearly covered at high-water, there was a big basin, known as the Kelpie's Pool, filled with sea-water and the loveliest sea-weed and many little sea-animals; and this was a favourite resort of the fairies. It was now, of course, crowded. When they saw his big head come peeping over, they burst into a loud fit of laughter, and began mocking him and making game of him in a hundred ways. Some made the ugliest faces they could, some queer gestures of contempt; others sung bits of songs, and so on; while the queen sat by herself on a projecting corner of the rock, with her feet in the water, and looked at him sulkily. Many of them kept on plunging and swimming and diving and floating, while they mocked him; and Colin would have enjoyed the sight much if they had not spoiled their beauty and their motions by their grimaces and their gestures.

"I want my child," said Colin.

"Give him his child," cried one.

Thereupon a dozen of them dived, and brought up a huge sea-slug—a horrid creature, like a lump of blubber—and held it up to him, saying—

"There he is; come down and fetch him."

Others offered him a blue lobster, struggling in their grasp; others, a spider-crab; others, a whelk; while some of them sung mocking verses, each capping the line the other gave. At length they lifted a dreadful object from the bottom. It was like a baby with his face half eaten away by the fishes, only that he had a huge nose, like the big toe of a lobster. But Colin was not to be taken in.

"Very well, good people," he said, "I will try something else."

He crept down the rock again, took out the little cobbler's awl, and began boring a hole. It went through the rock as if it had been butter, and as he drew it out the water followed in a far-reaching spout. He bored another, and went on boring till there were three hundred and thirteen spouts gushing from the rock, and running away in a strong little stream towards the sea. He then sat down on a ledge at the foot of the rock and waited.

By-and-by he heard a clamour of little voices from the basin. They had found that the water was getting very low. But when they discovered the holes by which it was escaping, "He's got Dottlecob's awl! He's got Dottlecob's awl!" they cried with one voice of horror. When he heard this, Colin climbed the rock again to enjoy their confusion. But here I must explain a little.

In the former part of this history I showed how fond these fairies were of water. But the fact was, they were far too fond of it. It had grown a thorough dissipation with them. Their business had been chiefly to tend and help the flowers in which they lived, and to do good offices for every thing that had any kind of life about them. Hence their name of Good People. But from finding the good the water did to the flowers, and from sharing in the refreshment it brought them, flowing up to them in tiny runnels through the veins of the plants, they had fallen in love with the water itself, for its own sake, or rather for the pleasure it gave to them, irrespective of the good it was to the flowers which lived upon it. So they neglected their business, and took to sailing on the streams, and plunging into every pool they could find. Hence the rapidity of their decline and fall.

Again, on coming to the sea-coast, they had found that the salt water did much to restore the beauty they had lost by partaking of the Carasoyn. Therefore they were constantly on the shore, bathing for ever in the water, especially that left in this pool by the ebbing tide, which was particularly to their taste; till at last they had grown entirely dependent for comfort on the sea-water, and, they thought, entirely dependent on it for existence also, at least such existence as was in the least worth possessing.

Therefore when they saw the big face of Colin peering once more over the ledge, they rushed at him in a rage, scrambling up the side of the rock like so many mad beetles. Colin drew back and let them come on. The moment the foremost put his foot on the line that Colin had drawn around the rock, he slipped and tumbled backwards head over heels into the pool, shrieking—

"He's got Dottlecob's wax!"

"He's got Dottlecob's wax!" screamed the next, as he fell backwards after his companion, and this took place till no one would approach the line. In fact no fairy could keep his footing on the wax, and the line was so broad—for as Colin rubbed it, it had melted and spread—that not one of them could spring over it. The queen now rose.

"What do you want, Colin?" she said.

"I want my child, as you know very well," answered Colin.

"Come and take him," returned the queen, and sat down again, not now with her feet in the water, for it was much too low for that.

But Colin knew better. He sat down on the edge of the basin. Unfortunately, the tail of his coat crossed the line. In a moment half-a-dozen of the fairies were out of the circle. Colin rose instantly, and there was not much harm done, for the multitude was still in prison. The water was nearly gone, beginning to leave the very roots of the long tangles uncovered. At length the queen could bear it no longer.

"Look here, Colin," she said; "I wish you well."

And as she spoke she rose and descended the side of the rock towards the water now far below her. She had to be very cautious too, the stones were so slippery, though there was none of Dottlecob's wax there. About half-way below where the surface of the pool had been, she stopped, and pushed a stone aside. Colin saw what seemed the entrance to a cave inside the rock. The queen went in. A few moments after she came out wringing her hands.

"Oh dear! oh dear! What shall I do?" she cried. "You horrid thick people will grow so. He's grown to such a size I *can't* get him out."

"Will you let him go if I get him out?" asked Colin.

"I will, I will. We shall all be starved to death for want of sea-water if I don't," she answered.

"Swear by the cobbler's awl and the cobbler's wax," said Colin.

"I swear," said the queen.

"By the cobbler's awl and the cobbler's wax," insisted Colin.

"I swear by the cobbler's awl and the cobbler's wax," returned the queen.

"In the name of your people?"

"In the name of my people," said the queen, "that none of us here present will ever annoy you or your family hereafter."

"Then I'll come down," said Colin, and jumped into the basin. With the cobbler's awl he soon cleared a big opening into the rock, for it bored and cut it like butter. Then out crept a beautiful boy of about ten years old, into his father's arms, with eyes, and ears, and chin, and cheek all safe and sound. And he carried him home to his mother.

It was a disappointment to find him so much of a baby at his age; but that fault soon began to mend. And the house was full of jubilation. And little Colin told them the whole story of his sojourn among the fairies. And it did not take so long as you would think, for he fancied he had been there only about a week.

Editor's Note:

This last story does not have the bleak, brooding atmosphere of *The Carasoyn;* it is filled with a lambent, glowing air of its own. It is dreamy and mystical, with a vague, dim, wondering beauty, and perhaps for these reasons it reminds me more of MacDonald's two great haunting dream-romances, *Lilith* and *Phantastes.*

The Golden Key first appeared in a book called *Dealings with the Fairies,* which was published in London by Strahan in 1867. Although only about 12,300 words in length, it is one of MacDonald's major works and is usually singled out as a brilliant achievement. C. S. Lewis, one of MacDonald's most fervent admirers among our contemporary writers, once said: "The great works are *Phantastes,* the Curdie books, *The Golden Key, The Wise Woman,* and *Lilith.*" The *Times Literary Supplement,* marking the centennial of MacDonald's birth, said in 1924: "The author of *The Golden Key* and of *Lilith* had a touch of genius."

To these judgments I can only agree, and suggest you go straight to the story.

The Golden Key

There was a boy who used to sit in the twilight and listen to his great-aunt's stories.

She told him that if he could reach the place where the end of the rainbow stands he would find there a golden key.

"And what is the key for?" the boy would ask. "What is it the key of? What will it open?"

"That nobody knows," his aunt would reply. "He has to find that out."

"I suppose, being gold," the boy once said, thoughtfully, "that I could get a good deal of money for it if I sold it."

"Better never find it than sell it," returned his aunt.

And then the boy went to bed and dreamed about the golden key.

Now all that his great-aunt told the boy about the golden key would have been nonsense, had it not been that their little house stood on the borders of Fairyland. For it is perfectly well known that out of Fairyland nobody ever can find where the rainbow stands. The creature takes such good care of its golden key, always flitting from place to place, lest any one should find it! But in Fairyland it is quite different. Things that look real in this country look very thin indeed in Fairyland, while some of the things that here cannot stand still for a moment, will not move there. So it was not in the least absurd of the old lady to tell her nephew such things about the golden key.

"Did you ever know anybody to find it?" he asked, one evening.

"Yes. Your father, I believe, found it."

"And what did he do with it, can you tell me?"

"He never told me."

"What was it like?"

"He never showed it to me."

"How does a new key come there always?"

"I don't know. There it is."

"Perhaps it is the rainbow's egg."

"Perhaps it is. You will be a happy boy if you find the nest."

"Perhaps it comes tumbling down the rainbow from the sky."

"Perhaps it does."

One evening, in summer, he went into his own room, and stood at the lattice-window, and gazed into the forest which fringed the outskirts of Fairyland. It came close up to his great-aunt's garden, and, indeed, sent some straggling trees into it. The forest lay to the east, and the sun, which was setting behind the cottage, looked straight into the dark wood with his level red eye. The trees were all old, and had few branches below, so that the sun could see a great way into the forest; and the boy, being keen-sighted, could see almost as far as the sun. The trunks stood like rows of red columns in the shine of the red sun, and he could see down aisle after aisle in the vanishing distance. And as he gazed into the forest he began to feel as if the trees were all waiting for him, and had something they could not go on with till he came to them. But he was hungry and wanted his supper. So he lingered.

Suddenly, far among the trees, as far as the sun could shine, he saw a glorious thing. It was the end of a rainbow, large and brilliant. He could count all seven colours, and could see shade after shade beyond the violet; while before the red stood a colour more gorgeous and mysterious still. It was a colour he had never seen before. Only the spring of the rainbow-arch was visible. He could see nothing of it above the trees.

"The golden key!" he said to himself, and darted out of the house, and into the wood.

He had not gone far before the sun set. But the rainbow only glowed the brighter. For the rainbow of Fairyland is not dependent upon the sun as ours is. The trees welcomed him. The bushes made way for him. The rainbow grew larger and brighter; and at length he found himself within two trees of it.

It was a grand sight, burning away there in silence, with its gorgeous, its lovely, its delicate colours, each distinct, all combining. He could now see a great deal more of it. It rose high into the blue heavens, but bent so little that he could not tell how high the crown of the arch must reach. It was still only a small portion of a huge bow.

He stood gazing at it till he forgot himself with delight—even forgot the key which he had come to seek. And as he stood it grew more wonderful still. For in each of the colours, which was as large as the column of a church, he could faintly see beautiful forms slowly ascending as if by the steps of a winding stair. The forms appeared irregularly —now one, now many, now several, now none— men and women and children—all different, all beautiful.

He drew nearer to the rainbow. It vanished. He started back a step in dismay. It was there again, as beautiful as ever. So he contented himself with standing as near it as he might, and watching the forms that ascended the glorious colours towards the unknown height of the arch, which did not end abruptly but faded away in the blue air, so gradually that he could not say where it ceased.

When the thought of the golden key returned, the boy very wisely proceeded to mark out in his mind the space covered by the foundation of the rainbow, in order that he might know where to search, should the rainbow disappear. It was based chiefly upon a bed of moss.

Meantime it had grown quite dark in the wood. The rainbow alone was visible by its own light. But the moment the moon rose the rainbow vanished. Nor could any change of place restore the vision to the boy's eyes. So he threw himself down upon the mossy bed, to wait till the sunlight would give him a chance of finding the key. There he fell fast asleep.

When he woke in the morning the sun was looking straight into his eyes. He turned away from it, and the same moment saw a brilliant little thing lying on the moss within a foot of his face. It was the golden key. The pipe of it was of plain gold, as bright as gold could be. The handle was curiously wrought and set with sapphires. In a terror of delight he put out his hand and took it, and had it.

He lay for a while, turning it over and over, and feeding his eyes upon its beauty. Then he jumped to his feet, remembering that the pretty thing was of no use to him yet. Where was the lock to which the key belonged? It must be somewhere, for how could anybody be so silly as make a key for which there was no lock? Where should he go to look for it? He gazed about him, up into the air, down to the earth, but saw no keyhole in the clouds, in the grass, or in the trees.

Just as he began to grow disconsolate, however, he saw something glimmering in the wood. It was a mere glimmer that he saw, but he took it for a glimmer of rainbow, and went towards it.—And now I will go back to the borders of the forest.

Not far from the house where the boy had lived,

there was another house, the owner of which was a merchant, who was much away from home. He had lost his wife some years before, and had only one child, a little girl, whom he left to the charge of two servants, who were very idle and careless. So she was neglected and left untidy, and was sometimes ill-used besides.

Now it is well known that the little creatures commonly called fairies, though there are many different kinds of fairies in Fairyland, have an exceeding dislike to untidiness. Indeed, they are quite spiteful to slovenly people. Being used to all the lovely ways of the trees and flowers, and to the neatness of the birds and all woodland creatures, it makes them feel miserable, even in their deep woods and on their grassy carpets, to think that within the same moonlight lies a dirty, uncomfortable, slovenly house. And this makes them angry with the people that live in it, and they would gladly drive them out of the world if they could. They want the whole earth nice and clean. So they pinch the maids black and blue, and play them all manner of uncomfortable tricks.

But this house was quite a shame, and the fairies in the forest could not endure it. They tried everything on the maids without effect, and at last resolved upon making a clean riddance, beginning with the child. They ought to have known that it was not her fault, but they have little principle and much mischief in them, and they thought that if they got rid of her the maids would be sure to be turned away.

So one evening, the poor little girl having been put to bed early, before the sun was down, the servants went off to the village, locking the door behind them. The child did not know she was alone, and lay contentedly looking out of her window towards the forest, of which, however, she could not see much, because of the ivy and other creeping plants which had straggled across her window. All at once she saw an ape making faces at her out of the mirror, and the heads carved upon a great old wardrobe grinning fearfully. Then two old spider-legged chairs came forward into the middle of the room, and began to dance a queer, old-fashioned dance. This set her laughing, and she forgot the ape and the grinning heads. So the fairies saw they had made a mistake, and sent the chairs back to their places. But they knew that she had been reading the story of Silverhair all day. So the next moment she heard the voices of the three bears upon the stair, big voice, middle voice, and little voice, and she heard their soft, heavy tread, as if they had had stockings over their boots, coming nearer and nearer to the door of her room, till she could bear it no longer. She did just as Silverhair did, and as the fairies wanted her to do: she darted to the window, pulled it open, got upon the ivy, and so scrambled to the ground. She then fled to the forest as fast as she could run.

Now, although she did not know it, this was the very best way she could have gone; for nothing is ever so mischievous in its own place as it is out of it; and, besides, these mischievous creatures were only the children of Fairyland, as it were, and there are many other beings there as well; and if a wanderer gets in among them, the good ones will always help him more than the evil ones will be able to hurt him.

The sun was now set, and the darkness coming on, but the child thought of no danger but the bears behind her. If she had looked round, however, she would have seen that she was followed by a very different creature from a bear. It was a curious creature, made like a fish, but covered, instead of scales, with feathers of all colours, sparkling like those of a hummingbird. It had fins, not wings, and swam through the air as a fish does through the water. Its head was like the head of a small owl.

After running a long way, and as the last of the light was disappearing, she passed under a tree with drooping branches. It dropped its branches to the ground all about her, and caught her as in a trap. She struggled to get out, but the branches pressed her closer and closer to the trunk. She was in great terror and distress, when the air-fish, swimming into the thicket of branches, began tearing them with its beak. They loosened their hold at once, and the creature went on attacking them, till at length they let the child go. Then the air-fish came from behind her, and swam on in front, glittering and sparkling all lovely colours; and she followed.

It led her gently along till all at once it swam in at a cottage-door. The child followed still. There was a bright fire in the middle of the floor, upon which stood a pot without a lid, full of water that boiled and bubbled furiously. The air-fish swam straight to the pot and into the boiling water, where it lay quiet. A beautiful woman rose from the opposite side of the fire and came to meet the girl. She took her up in her arms, and said,—

"Ah, you are come at last! I have been looking for you a long time."

She sat down with her on her lap, and there the girl sat staring at her. She had never seen anything so beautiful. She was tall and strong, with white arms and neck, and a delicate flush on her face. The child could not tell what was the colour of her hair, but could not help thinking it had a tinge of dark green. She had not one ornament upon her, but she looked as if she had just put off quantities of diamonds and emeralds. Yet here she was in the simplest, poorest little cottage, where she was evidently at home. She was dressed in shining green.

The girl looked at the lady, and the lady looked at the girl.

"What is your name?" asked the lady.

"The servants always called me Tangle."

"Ah, that was because your hair was so untidy. But that was their fault, the naughty women! Still it is a pretty name, and I will call you Tangle too. You must not mind my asking you questions, for you may ask me the same questions, every one of them, and any others that you like. How old are you?"

"Ten," answered Tangle.

"You don't look like it," said the lady.

"How old are you, please?" returned Tangle.

"Thousands of years old," answered the lady.

"You don't look like it," said Tangle.

"Don't I? I think I do. Don't you see how beautiful I am!"

And her great blue eyes looked down on the little Tangle, as if all the stars in the sky were melted in them to make their brightness.

"Ah! but," said Tangle, "when people live long they grow old. At least I always thought so."

"I have not time to grow old," said the lady. "I am too busy for that. It is very idle to grow old. —But I cannot have my little girl so untidy. Do you know I can't find a clean spot on your face to kiss!"

"Perhaps," suggested Tangle, feeling ashamed, but not too much so to say a word for herself—"perhaps that is because the tree made me cry so."

"My poor darling!" said the lady, looking now as if the moon were melted in her eyes, and kissing her little face, dirty as it was, "the naughty tree must suffer for making a girl cry."

"And what is your name, please?" asked Tangle.

"Grandmother," answered the lady.

"Is it really?"

"Yes, indeed. I never tell stories, even in fun."

"How good of you!"

"I couldn't if I tried. It would come true if I said it, and then I should be punished enough."

And she smiled like the sun through a summer-shower.

"But now," she went on, "I must get you washed and dressed, and then we shall have some supper."

"Oh! I had supper long ago," said Tangle.

"Yes, indeed you had," answered the lady—"three years ago. You don't know that it is three years since you ran away from the bears. You are thirteen and more now."

Tangle could only stare. She felt quite sure it was true.

"You will not be afraid of anything I do with you—will you?" said the lady.

"I will try very hard not to be; but I can't be certain, you know," replied Tangle.

"I like your saying so, and I shall be quite satisfied," answered the lady.

She took off the girl's night-gown, rose with her in her arms, and going to the wall of the cottage, opened a door. Then Tangle saw a deep tank, the sides of which were filled with green plants, which had flowers of all colours. There was a roof over it like the roof of the cottage. It was filled with beautiful clear water, in which swam a multitude of such fishes as the one that had led her to the cottage. It was the light their colours gave that showed the place in which they were.

The lady spoke some words Tangle could not understand, and threw her into the tank

The fishes came crowding about her. Two or three of them got under her head and kept it up. The rest of them rubbed themselves all over her, and with their wet feathers washed her quite clean. Then the lady, who had been looking on all the time, spoke again; whereupon some thirty or forty of the fishes rose out of the water underneath Tangle, and so bore her up to the arms the lady held out to take her. She carried her back to the fire, and, having dried her well, opened a chest, and taking out the finest linen garments, smelling of grass and lavender, put them upon her, and over all a green dress, just like her own, shining like hers, and soft like hers, and going into just such lovely folds from the waist, where it was tied with a brown cord, to her bare feet.

"Won't you give me a pair of shoes too, grandmother?" said Tangle.

"No, my dear; no shoes. Look here. I wear no shoes."

So saying she lifted her dress a little, and there were the loveliest white feet, but no shoes. Then Tangle was content to go without shoes too. And the lady sat down with her again, and combed her hair, and brushed it, and then left it to dry while she got the supper.

First she got bread out of one hole in the wall; then milk out of another; then several kinds of fruit out a third; and then she went to the pot on the fire, and took out the fish, now nicely cooked, and, as soon as she had pulled off its feathered skin, ready to be eaten.

"But," exclaimed Tangle. And she stared at the fish, and could say no more.

"I know what you mean," returned the lady. "You do not like to eat the messenger that brought you home. But it is the kindest return you can make. The creature was afraid to go until it saw me put the pot on, and heard me promise it should be boiled the moment it returned with you. Then it darted out of the door at once. You saw it go into the pot of itself the moment it entered, did you not?"

"I did," answered Tangle, "and I thought it very strange; but then I saw you, and forgot all about the fish."

"In Fairyland," resumed the lady, as they sat down to the table, "the ambition of the animals is to be eaten by the people; for that is their highest end in that condition. But they are not therefore destroyed. Out of that pot comes something more than the dead fish, you will see."

Tangle now remarked that the lid was on the pot. But the lady took no further notice of it till they had eaten the fish, which Tangle found nicer than any fish she had ever tasted before. It was as white as snow, and as delicate as cream. And the moment she had swallowed a mouthful of it, a change she could not describe began to take place in her. She heard a murmuring all about her, which became more and more articulate, and at length, as she went on eating, grew intelligible. By the time she had finished her share, the sounds of all the animals in the forest came crowding through the door to her ears; for the door still stood wide open, though it was pitch-dark outside; and they were no longer sounds only; they were speech, and speech that she could understand. She could tell what the insects in the cottage were saying to each other too. She had even a suspicion that the trees and flowers all about the cottage were holding midnight communications with each other; but what they said she could not hear.

As soon as the fish was eaten, the lady went to the fire and took the lid off the pot. A lovely little creature in human shape, with large white wings, rose out of it, and flew round and round the roof of the cottage; then dropped, fluttering, and nestled in the lap of the lady. She spoke to it some strange words, carried it to the door, and threw it out into the darkness. Tangle heard the flapping of its wings die away in the distance.

"Now have we done the fish any harm?" she said, returning.

"No," answered Tangle, "I do not think we have. I should not mind eating one every day."

"They must wait their time, like you and me too, my little Tangle."

And she smiled a smile made more lovely by the sadness in it.

"But," she continued, "I think we may have one for supper to-morrow."

So saying she went to the door of the tank, and spoke; and now Tangle understood her perfectly.

"I want one of you," she said,—"the wisest."

Thereupon the fishes got together in the middle of the tank, with their heads forming a circle above the water, and their tails a larger circle beneath it. They were holding a council, in which their relative wisdom should be determined. At length one of them flew up into the lady's hand, looking lively and ready.

"You know where the rainbow stands?" she asked.

"Yes, mother, quite well," answered the fish.

"Bring home a young man you will find there, who does not know where to go."

The fish was out of the door in a moment. Then the lady told Tangle it was time to go to bed; and, opening another door in the side of the cottage, showed her a little arbour, cool and green, with a bed of purple heath growing in it, upon which she threw a large wrapper made of the feathered skins of the wise fishes, shining gorgeous in the firelight. Tangle was soon lost in the strangest, loveliest dreams. And the beautiful lady was in every one of her dreams.

In the morning she woke to the rustling of leaves

over her head, and the sound of running water. But, to her surprise, she could find no door—nothing but the moss-grown wall of the cottage. So she crept through an opening in the arbour, and stood in the forest. Then she bathed in a stream that ran merrily through the trees, and felt happier; for having once been in her grandmother's pond, she must be clean and tidy ever after; and, having put on her green dress, felt like a lady.

She spent that day in the wood, listening to the birds and beasts and creeping things. She understood all that they said, though she could not repeat a word of it; and every kind had a different language, while there was a common though more limited understanding between all the inhabitants of the forest. She saw nothing of the beautiful lady, but she felt that she was near her all the time; and she took care not to go out of sight of the cottage. It was round, like a snow-hut or a wigwam; and she could see neither door nor window in it. The fact was, it had no windows; and though it was full of doors, they all opened from the inside, and could not even be seen from the outside.

She was standing at the foot of a tree in the twilight, listening to a quarrel between a mole and a squirrel, in which the mole told the squirrel that the tail was the best of him, and the squirrel called the mole Spade-fists, when, the darkness having deepened around her, she became aware of something shining in her face; and looking round, saw that the door of the cottage was open, and the red light of the fire flowing from it like a river through the darkness. She left Mole and Squirrel to settle matters as they might, and darted off to the cottage. Entering, she found the pot boiling on the fire, and the grand, lovely lady sitting on the other side of it.

"I've been watching you all day," said the lady.

"You shall have something to eat by-and-by, but we must wait till our supper comes home."

She took Tangle on her knee, and began to sing to her—such songs as made her wish she could listen to them for ever. But at length in rushed the shining fish, and snuggled down in the pot. It was followed by a youth who had outgrown his worn garments. His face was ruddy with health, and in his hand he carried a little jewel, which sparkled in the firelight.

The first words the lady said were,—

"What is that in your hand, Mossy?"

Now Mossy was the name his companions had given him, because he had a favourite stone covered with moss, on which he used to sit whole days reading; and they said the moss had begun to grow upon him too.

Mossy held out his hand. The moment the lady saw that it was the golden key, she rose from her chair, kissed Mossy on the forehead, made him sit down on her seat, and stood before him like a servant. Mossy could not bear this, and rose at once. But the lady begged him, with tears in her beautiful eyes, to sit, and let her wait on him.

"But you are a great, splendid, beautiful lady," said Mossy.

"Yes, I am. But I work all day long—that is my pleasure; and you will have to leave me so soon!"

"How do you know that, if you please, madam?" asked Mossy.

"Because you have got the golden key."

"But I don't know what it is for. I can't find the key-hole. Will you tell me what to do?"

"You must look for the key-hole. That is your work. I cannot help you. I can only tell you that if you look for it you will find it."

"What kind of box will it open? What is there inside?"

"I do not know. I dream about it, but I know nothing."

"Must I go at once?"

"You may stop here to-night, and have some of my supper. But you must go in the morning. All I can do for you is to give you clothes. Here is a girl called Tangle, whom you must take with you."

"That *will* be nice," said Mossy.

"No, no!" said Tangle. "I don't want to leave you, please, grandmother."

"You must go with him, Tangle. I am sorry to lose you, but it will be the best thing for you. Even the fishes, you see, have to go into the pot, and then out into the dark. If you fall in with the Old Man of the Sea, mind you ask him whether he has not got some more fishes ready for me. My tank is getting thin."

So saying, she took the fish from the pot, and put the lid on as before. They sat down and ate the fish, and then the winged creature rose from the pot, circled the roof, and settled on the lady's lap. She talked to it, carried it to the door, and threw it out into the dark. They heard the flap of its wings die away in the distance.

The lady then showed Mossy into just such another chamber as that of Tangle; and in the morning he found a suit of clothes laid beside him. He looked very handsome in them. But the wearer of Grandmother's clothes never thinks about how he or she looks, but thinks always how handsome other people are.

Tangle was very unwilling to go.

"Why should I leave you? I don't know the young man," she said to the lady.

"I am never allowed to keep my children long.

You need not go with him except you please, but you must go some day; and I should like you to go with him, for he has the golden key. No girl need be afraid to go with a youth that has the golden key. You will take care of her, Mossy, will you not?"

"That I will," said Mossy.

And Tangle cast a glance at him, and thought she should like to go with him.

"And," said the lady, "If you should lose each other as you go through the—the—I never can remember the name of that country,—do not be afraid, but go on and on."

She kissed Tangle on the mouth and Mossy on the forehead, led them to the door, and waved her hand eastward. Mossy and Tangle took each other's hand and walked away into the depth of the forest. In his right hand Mossy held the golden key.

They wandered thus a long way, with endless amusement from the talk of the animals. They soon learned enough of their language to ask them necessary questions. The squirrels were always friendly, and gave them nuts out of their own hoards; but the bees were selfish and rude, justifying themselves on the ground that Tangle and Mossy were not subjects of their queen, and charity must begin at home, though indeed they had not one drone in their poorhouse at the time. Even the blinking moles would fetch them an earth-nut or a truffle now and then, talking as if their mouths, as well as their eyes and ears, were full of cotton wool, or their own velvety fur. By the time they got out of the forest they were very fond of each other, and Tangle was not in the least sorry that her grandmother had sent her away with Mossy.

At length the trees grew smaller, and stood farther apart, and the ground began to rise, and it got more and more steep, till the trees were all left behind, and the two were climbing a narrow path with rocks on each side. Suddenly they came upon a rude doorway, by which they entered a narrow gallery cut in the rock. It grew darker and darker, till it was pitch-dark, and they had to feel their way. At length the light began to return, and at last they came out upon a narrow path on the face of a lofty precipice. This path went winding down the rock to a wide plain, circular in shape, and surrounded on all sides by mountains. Those opposite to them were a great way off, and towered to an awful height, shooting up sharp, blue, ice-enamelled pinnacles. An utter silence reigned where they stood. Not even the sound of water reached them.

Looking down, they could not tell whether the valley below was a grassy plain or a great still lake. They had never seen any place look like it. The way to it was difficult and dangerous, but down the narrow path they went, and reached the bottom in safety. They found it composed of smooth, light-coloured sandstone, undulating in parts, but mostly level. It was no wonder to them now that they had not been able to tell what it was, for this surface was everywhere crowded with shadows. It was a sea of shadows. The mass was chiefly made up of the shadows of leaves innumerable, of all lovely and imaginative forms, waving to and fro, floating and quivering in the breath of a breeze whose motion was unfelt, whose sound was unheard. No forests clothed the mountain-sides, no trees were anywhere to be seen, and yet the shadows of the leaves, branches, and stems of all various trees covered the valley as far as their eyes could reach. They soon spied the shadows of flowers mingled with those of the leaves, and now and then the shadow of a bird with open beak, and throat distended with song. At times would appear the forms of strange, graceful creatures, running up and down the shadow-boles and along the branches, to disappear in the wind-tossed foliage. As they walked they waded knee-deep in the lovely lake. For the shadows were not merely lying on the surface of the ground, but heaped up above it like substantial forms of darkness, as if they had been cast upon a thousand different planes of the air. Tangle and Mossy often lifted their heads and gazed upwards to descry whence the shadows came; but they could see nothing more than a bright mist spread above them, higher than the tops of the mountains, which stood clear against it. No forests, no leaves, no birds were visible.

After a while, they reached more open spaces, where the shadows were thinner; and came even to portions over which shadows only flitted, leaving them clear for such as might follow. Now a wonderful form, half bird-like half human, would float across on outspread sailing pinions. Anon an exquisite shadow group of gambolling children would be followed by the loveliest female form, and that again by the grand stride of a Titanic shape, each disappearing in the surrounding press of shadowy foliage. Sometimes a profile of unspeakable beauty or grandeur would appear for a moment and vanish. Sometimes they seemed lovers that passed linked arm in arm, sometimes father and son, sometimes brothers in loving contest, sometimes sisters entwined in gracefullest community of complex form. Sometimes wild horses would tear across, free, or bestrode by noble shadows of ruling men. But some of the things which pleased them most they never knew how to describe.

About the middle of the plain they sat down to rest in the heart of a heap of shadows. After sitting for a while, each, looking up, saw the other in tears: they were each longing after the country whence the shadows fell.

"We *must* find the country from which the shadows come," said Mossy.

"We must, dear Mossy," responded Tangle. "What if your golden key should be the key to *it?*"

"Ah! that would be grand," returned Mossy.— "But we must rest here for a little, and then we shall be able to cross the plain before night."

So he lay down on the ground, and about him on every side, and over his head, was the constant play of the wonderful shadows. He could look through them, and see the one behind the other, till they mixed in a mass of darkness. Tangle, too, lay admiring, and wondering, and longing after the country whence the shadows came. When they were rested they rose and pursued their journey.

How long they were in crossing this plain I cannot tell; but before night Mossy's hair was streaked with grey, and Tangle had got wrinkles on her forehead.

As evening drew on, the shadows fell deeper and rose higher. At length they reached a place where they rose above their heads, and made all dark around them. Then they took hold of each other's hand, and walked on in silence and in some dismay. They felt the gathering darkness, and something strangely solemn besides, and the beauty of the shadows ceased to delight them. All at once Tangle found that she had not a hold of Mossy's hand, though when she lost it she could not tell.

"Mossy, Mossy!" she cried aloud in terror.

But no Mossy replied.

A moment after, the shadows sank to her feet, and down under her feet, and the mountains rose before her. She turned towards the gloomy region she had left, and called once more upon Mossy. There the gloom lay tossing and heaving, a dark stormy, foamless sea of shadows, but no Mossy rose out of it, or came climbing up the hill on which she stood. She threw herself down and wept in despair.

Suddenly she remembered that the beautiful lady had told them, if they lost each other in a country of which she could not remember the name, they were not to be afraid, but to go straight on.

"And besides," she said to herself, "Mossy has the golden key, and so no harm will come to him, I do believe."

She rose from the ground, and went on.

Before long she arrived at a precipice, in the face of which a stair was cut. When she had ascended half-way, the stair ceased, and the path led straight into the mountain. She was afraid to enter, and turning again towards the stair, grew giddy at sight of the depth beneath her, and was forced to throw herself down in the mouth of the cave.

When she opened her eyes, she saw a beautiful little creature with wings standing beside her, waiting.

"I know you," said Tangle. "You are my fish."

"Yes. But I am a fish no longer. I am an aëranth now."

"What is that?" asked Tangle.

"What you see I am," answered the shape. "And I am come to lead you through the mountain."

"Oh! thank you, dear fish—aëranth, I mean," returned Tangle, rising.

Thereupon the aëranth took to his wings, and flew on through the long, narrow passage, reminding Tangle very much of the way he had swum on before her when he was a fish. And the moment his white wings moved, they began to throw off a continuous shower of sparks of all colours, which lighted up the passage before them.—All at once he vanished, and Tangle heard a low, sweet sound, quite different from the rush and crackle of his wings. Before her was an open arch, and through it came light, mixed with the sound of sea-waves.

She hurried out, and fell, tired and happy, upon the yellow sand of the shore. There she lay, half asleep with weariness and rest, listening to the low plash and retreat of the tiny waves, which seemed ever enticing the land to leave off being land, and become sea. And as she lay, her eyes were fixed upon the foot of a great rainbow standing far away against the sky on the other side of the sea. At length she fell fast asleep.

When she awoke, she saw an old man with long white hair down to his shoulders, leaning upon a stick covered with green buds, and so bending over her.

"What do you want here, beautiful woman?" he said.

"Am I beautiful? I am so glad!" answered Tangle, rising. "My grandmother is beautiful."

"Yes. But what do you want?" he repeated, kindly.

"I think I want you. Are not you the Old Man of the Sea?"

"I am."

"Then grandmother says, have you any more fishes ready for her?"

"We will go and see, my dear," answered the old man, speaking yet more kindly than before. "And I can do something for you, can I not?"

"Yes—show me the way up to the country from which the shadows fall," said Tangle.

For there she hoped to find Mossy again.

"Ah! indeed, that would be worth doing," said the old man. "But I cannot, for I do not know the way myself. But I will send you to the Old Man of the Earth. Perhaps he can tell you. He is much older than I am."

Leaning on his staff, he conducted her along the

shore to a steep rock, that looked like a petrified ship turned upside down. The door of it was the rudder of a great vessel, ages ago at the bottom of the sea. Immediately within the door was a stair in the rock, down which the old man went, and Tangle followed. At the bottom the old man had his house, and there he lived.

As soon as she entered it, Tangle heard a strange noise, unlike anything she had ever heard before. She soon found that it was the fishes talking. She tried to understand what they said; but their speech was so old-fashioned, and rude, and undefined, that she could not make much of it.

"I will go and see about those fishes for my daughter," said the Old Man of the Sea.

And moving a slide in the wall of his house, he first looked out, and then tapped upon a thick piece of crystal that filled the round opening. Tangle came up behind him, and peeping through the window into the heart of the great deep green ocean, saw the most curious creatures, some very ugly, all very odd, and with especially queer mouths, swimming about everywhere, above and below, but all coming towards the window in answer to the tap of the Old Man of the Sea. Only a few could get their mouths against the glass; but those who were floating miles away yet turned their heads towards it. The Old Man looked through the whole flock carefully for some minutes, and then turning to Tangle, said,—

"I am sorry I have not got one ready yet. I want more time than she does. But I will send some as soon as I can."

He then shut the slide.

Presently a great noise arose in the sea. The old man opened the slide again, and tapped on the glass, whereupon the fishes were all as still as sleep.

"They were only talking about you," he said. "And they do speak such nonsense!—To-morrow," he continued, "I must show you the way to the Old Man of the Earth. He lives a long way from here."

"Do let me go at once," said Tangle.

"No. That is not possible. You must come this way first."

He led her to a hole in the wall, which she had not observed before. It was covered with the green leaves and white blossoms of a creeping plant.

"Only white-blossoming plants can grow under the sea," said the old man. "In there you will find a bath, in which you must lie till I call you."

Tangle went in, and found a smaller room or cave, in the further corner of which was a great basin hollowed out of a rock, and half full of the clearest sea-water. Little streams were constantly running into it from cracks in the wall of the cavern. It was polished quite smooth inside, and had a carpet of yellow sand in the bottom of it. Large green leaves and white flowers of various plants crowded up and over it, draping and covering it almost entirely.

No sooner was she undressed and lying in the bath, than she began to feel as if the water were sinking into her, and she was receiving all the good of sleep without undergoing its forgetfulness. She felt the good coming all the time. And she grew happier and more hopeful than she had been since she lost Mossy. But she could not help thinking how very sad it was for a poor old man to live there all alone, and have to take care of a whole seaful of stupid and riotous fishes.

After about an hour, as she thought, she heard his voice calling her, and rose out of the bath. All the fatigue and aching of her long journey had vanished. She was as whole, and strong, and well as if she had slept for seven days.

Returning to the opening that led into the other part of the house, she started back with amazement, for through it she saw the form of a grand man, with a majestic and beautiful face, waiting for her.

"Come," he said; "I see you are ready."

She entered with reverence.

"Where is the Old Man of the Sea?" she asked, humbly.

"There is no one here but me," he answered, smiling. "Some people call me the Old Man of the Sea. Others have another name for me, and are terribly frightened when they meet me taking a walk by the shore. Therefore I avoid being seen by them, for they are so afraid, that they never see what I really am. You see me now.—But I must show you the way to the Old Man of the Earth."

He led her into the cave where the bath was, and there she saw, in the opposite corner, a second opening in the rock.

"Go down that stair, and it will bring you to him," said the Old Man of the Sea.

With humble thanks Tangle took her leave. She went down the winding-stair, till she began to fear there was no end to it. Still down and down it went, rough and broken, with springs of water bursting out of the rocks and running down the steps beside her. It was quite dark about her, and yet she could see. For after being in that bath, people's eyes always give out a light they can see by. There were no creeping things in the way. All was safe and pleasant though so dark and damp and deep.

At last there was not one step more, and she found herself in a glimmering cave. On a stone in the middle of it sat a figure with its back towards her—the figure of an old man bent double with age. From behind she could see his white beard spread out on the rocky floor in front of him. He did not move as she entered, so she passed round that she might stand before him and speak to him. The moment she looked in his face, she saw that he was

a youth of marvellous beauty. He sat entranced with
the delight of what he beheld in a mirror of something like silver, which lay on the floor at his feet,
and which from behind she had taken for his white
beard. He sat on, heedless of her presence, pale with
the joy of his vision. She stood and watched him. At
length, all trembling, she spoke. But her voice made
no sound. Yet the youth lifted up his head. He
showed no surprise, however, at seeing her—only
smiled a welcome.

"Are you the Old Man of the Earth?" Tangle
had said.

And the youth answered, and Tangle heard him,
though not with her ears:—

"I am. What can I do for you?"

"Tell me the way to the country whence the shadows fall."

"Ah! that I do not know. I only dream about it
myself. I see its shadows sometimes in my mirror:
the way to it I do not know. But I think the Old
Man of the Fire must know. He is much older than
I am. He is the oldest man of all."

"Where does he live?"

"I will show you the way to his place. I never
saw him myself."

So saying, the young man rose, and then stood
for a while gazing at Tangle.

"I wish I could see that country too," he said.
"But I must mind my work."

He led her to the side of the cave, and told her
to lay her ear against the wall.

"What do you hear?" he asked.

"I hear," answered Tangle, "the sound of a great
water running inside the rock."

"That river runs down to the dwelling of the
oldest man of all—the Old Man of the Fire. I wish
I could go to see him. But I must mind my work.
That river is the only way to him."

Then the Old Man of the Earth stooped over the floor of the cave, raised a huge stone from it, and left it leaning. It disclosed a great hole that went plumb-down.

"That is the way," he said.

"But there are no stairs."

"You must throw yourself in. There is no other way."

She turned and looked him full in the face—stood so for a whole minute, as she thought: it was a whole year—then threw herself headlong into the hole.

When she came to herself, she found herself gliding down fast and deep. Her head was under water, but that did not signify, for, when she thought about it, she could not remember that she had breathed once since her bath in the cave of the Old Man of the Sea. When she lifted up her head a sudden and fierce heat struck her, and she sank it again instantly, and went sweeping on.

Gradually the stream grew shallower. At length she could hardly keep her head under. Then the water could carry her no farther. She rose from the channel, and went step for step down the burning descent. The water ceased altogether. The heat was terrible. She felt scorched to the bone, but it did not touch her strength. It grew hotter and hotter. She said, "I can bear it no longer." Yet she went on.

At the long last, the stair ended at a rude archway in an all but glowing rock. Through this archway Tangle fell exhausted into a cool mossy cave. The floor and walls were covered with moss—green, soft, and damp. A little stream spouted from a rent in the rock and fell into a basin of moss. She plunged her face into it and drank. Then she lifted her head and looked around. Then she rose and looked again. She saw no one in the cave. But the

moment she stood upright she had a marvellous
sense that she was in the secret of the earth and all
its ways. Everything she had seen, or learned from
books; all that her grandmother had said or sung
to her; all the talk of the beasts, birds, and fishes;
all that had happened to her on her journey with
Mossy, and since then in the heart of the earth
with the Old man and the Older man—all was plain:
she understood it all, and saw that everything meant
the same thing, though she could not have put it
into words again.

The next moment she descried, in a corner of
the cave, a little naked child, sitting on the moss.
He was playing with balls of various colours and
sizes, which he disposed in strange figures upon
the floor beside him. And now Tangle felt that there
was something in her knowledge which was not in
her understanding. For she knew there must be an
infinite meaning in the change and sequence and
individual forms of the figures into which the child
arranged the balls, as well as in the varied harmonies
of their colours, but what it all meant she could
not tell.* He went on busily, tirelessly, playing his
solitary game, without looking up, or seeming to
know that there was a stranger in his deep-with-
drawn cell. Diligently as a lace-maker shifts her
bobbins, he shifted and arranged his balls. Flashes
of meaning would now pass from them to Tangle,
and now again all would be not merely obscure,
but utterly dark. She stood looking for a long time,
for there was fascination in the sight; and the longer
she looked the more an indescribable vague intel-
ligence went on rousing itself in her mind. For
seven years she had stood there watching the naked
child with his coloured balls, and it seemed to her

*I think I must be indebted to Novalis for these geo-
metrical figures.

like seven hours, when all at once the shape the balls took, she knew not why, reminded her of the Valley of Shadows, and she spoke:—

"Where is the Old Man of the Fire?" she said.

"Here I am," answered the child, rising and leaving his balls on the moss. "What can I do for you?"

There was such an awfulness of absolute repose on the face of the child that Tangle stood dumb before him. He had no smile, but the love in his large grey eyes was deep as the centre. And with the repose there lay on his face a shimmer as of moonlight, which seemed as if any moment it might break into such a ravishing smile as would cause the beholder to weep himself to death. But the smile never came, and the moonlight lay there unbroken. For the heart of the child was too deep for any smile to reach from it to his face.

"Are you the oldest man of all?" Tangle at length, although filled with awe, ventured to ask.

"Yes, I am. I am very, very old. I am able to help you, I know. I can help everybody."

And the child drew near and looked up in her face so that she burst into tears.

"Can you tell me the way to the country the shadows fall from?" she sobbed.

"Yes. I know the way quite well. I go there myself sometimes. But you could not go my way; you are not old enough. I will show you how you can go."

"Do not send me out into the great heat again," prayed Tangle.

"I will not," answered the child.

And he reached up, and put his little cool hand on her heart.

"Now," he said, "you can go. The fire will not burn you. Come."

He led her from the cave, and following him through another archway, she found herself in a vast desert of sand and rock. The sky of it was of rock, lowering over than like solid thunderclouds; and the whole place was so hot that she saw, in bright rivulets, the yellow gold and white silver and red copper trickling molten from the rocks. But the heat never came near her.

When they had gone some distance, the child turned up a great stone, and took something like an egg from under it. He next drew a long curved line in the sand with his finger, and laid the egg in it. He then spoke something Tangle could not understand. The egg broke, a small snake came out, and, lying in the line in the sand, grew and grew till he filled it. The moment he was thus full-grown, he began to glide away, undulating like a sea-wave.

"Follow that serpent," said the child. "He will lead you the right way."

Tangle followed the serpent. But she could not go far without looking back at the marvellous Child. He stood alone in the midst of the glowing desert, beside a fountain of red flame that had burst forth at his feet, his naked whiteness glimmering a pale rosy red in the torrid fire. There he stood, looking after her, till, from the lengthening distance, she could see him no more. The serpent went straight on, turning neither to the right nor left.

Meantime Mossy had got out of the lake of shadows, and, following his mournful, lonely way, had reached the sea-shore. It was a dark, stormy evening. The sun had set. The wind was blowing from the sea. The waves had surrounded the rock within which lay the Old Man's house. A deep water rolled between it and the shore, upon which a majestic figure was walking alone.

Mossy went up to him and said,—

"Will you tell me where to find the Old Man of the Sea?"

"I am the Old Man of the Sea," the figure answered.

"I see a strong kingly man of middle age," returned Mossy.

Then the Old Man looked at him more intently, and said,—

"Your sight, young man, is better than that of most who take this way. The night is stormy: come to my house and tell me what I can do for you."

Mossy followed him. The waves flew from before the footsteps of the Old Man of the Sea, and Mossy followed upon dry sand.

When they had reached the cave, they sat down and gazed at each other.

Now Mossy was an old man by this time. He looked much older than the Old Man of the Sea, and his feet were very weary.

After looking at him for a moment, the Old Man took him by the hand and led him into his inner cave. There he helped him to undress, and laid him in the bath. And he saw that one of his hands Mossy did not open.

"What have you in that hand?" he asked.

Mossy opened his hand, and there lay the golden key.

"Ah!" said the Old Man, "that accounts for your knowing me. And I know the way you have to go."

"I want to find the country whence the shadows fall," said Mossy.

"I dare say you do. So do I. But meantime, one thing is certain.—What is that key for, do you think?"

"For a keyhole somewhere. But I don't know why I keep it. I never could find the keyhole. And I have lived a good while, I believe," said Mossy, sadly. "I'm not sure that I'm not old. I know my feet ache."

"Do they?" said the Old Man, as if he really

meant to ask the question; and Mossy, who was still lying in the bath, watched his feet for a moment before he replied,

"No, they do not," he answered. "Perhaps I am not old either."

"Get up and look at yourself in the water."

He rose and looked at himself in the water, and there was not a grey hair on his head or a wrinkle on his skin.

"You have tasted of death now," said the Old Man. "Is it good?"

"It is good," said Mossy. "It is better than life."

"No," said the Old Man: "it is only more life. —Your feet will make no holes in the water now."

"What do you mean?"

"I will show you that presently."

They returned to the outer cave, and sat and talked together for a long time. At length the Old Man of the Sea rose, and said to Mossy,—

"Follow me."

He let him up the stair again, and opened another door. They stood on the level of the raging sea, looking towards the east. Across the waste of waters, against the bosom of a fierce black cloud, stood the foot of a rainbow, glowing in the dark.

"This indeed is my way," said Mossy, as soon as he saw the rainbow, and stepped out upon the sea. His feet made no holes in the water. He fought the wind, and clomb the waves, and went on towards the rainbow.

The storm died away. A lovely day and a lovelier night followed. A cool wind blew over the wide plain of the quiet ocean. And still Mossy journeyed eastward. But the rainbow had vanished with the storm.

Day after day he held on, and he thought he had no guide. He did not see how a shining fish under the waters directed his steps. He crossed the sea, and came to a great precipice of rock, up which he could discover but one path. Nor did this lead him farther than half-way up the rock, where it ended on a platform. Here he stood and pondered. —It could not be that the way stopped here, else what was the path for? It was a rough path, not very plain, yet certainly a path.—He examined the face of the rock. It was smooth as glass. But as his eyes kept roving hopelessly over it, something glittered, and he caught sight of a row of small sapphires. They bordered a little hole in the rock.

"The keyhole!" he cried.

He tried the key. It fitted. It turned. A great clang and clash, as of iron bolts on huge brazen caldrons, echoed thunderously within. He drew out the key. The rock in front of him began to fall. He retreated from it as far as the breadth of the platform would allow. A great slab fell at his feet. In front was still the solid rock, with this one slab fallen forward out of it. But the moment he stepped upon it, a second fell, just short of the edge of the first, making the next step of a stair, which thus kept dropping itself before him as he ascended into the heart of the precipice. It led him into a hall fit for such an approach—irregular and rude in formation, but floor, sides, pillars, and vaulted roof, all one mass of shining stones of every colour that light can show. In the centre stood seven columns, ranged from red to violet. And on the pedestal of one of them sat a woman, motionless, with her face bowed upon her knees. Seven years had she sat there waiting. She lifted her head as Mossy drew near. It was Tangle. Her hair had grown to her feet, and was rippled like the windless sea on broad sands. Her face was beautiful, like her grandmother's, and as still and peaceful as that of the Old Man of the Fire. Her form was tall and noble. Yet Mossy knew her at once.

"How beautiful you are, Tangle!" he said, in delight and astonishment.

"Am I?" she returned. "Oh, I have waited for you so long! But you, you are the Old Man of the Sea. No. You are like the Old Man of the Earth. No, no. You are like the oldest man of all. You are like them all. And yet you are my own old Mossy! How did you come here? What did you do after I lost you? Did you find the keyhole? Have you got the key still?"

She had a hundred questions to ask him, and he a hundred more to ask her. They told each other all their adventures, and were as happy as man and woman could be. For they were younger and better, and stronger and wiser, than they had ever been before.

It began to grow dark. And they wanted more than ever to reach the country whence the shadows fall. So they looked about them for a way out of the cave. The door by which Mossy entered had closed again, and there was half a mile of rock between them and the sea. Neither could Tangle find the opening in the floor by which the serpent had led her thither. They searched till it grew so dark that they could see nothing, and gave it up.

After a while, however, the cave began to glimmer again. The light came from the moon, but it did not look like moonlight, for it gleamed through those seven pillars in the middle, and filled the place with all colours. And now Mossy saw that there was a pillar beside the red one, which he had not observed before. And it was of the same new colour that he had seen in the rainbow when he saw it first in the fairy forest. And on it he saw a sparkle of blue. It was the sapphires round the keyhole.

He took his key. It turned in the lock to the sounds of Æolian music. A door opened upon slow hinges, and disclosed a winding stair within. The key vanished from his fingers. Tangle went up. Mossy followed. The door closed behind them. They climbed out of the earth; and, still climbing, rose above it. They were in the rainbow. Far abroad, over ocean and land, they could see through its transparent walls the earth beneath their feet. Stairs beside stairs wound up together, and beautiful beings of all ages climbed along with them.

They knew that they were going up to the country whence the shadows fall.

And by this time I think they must have got there.